In her impressive debut novel, *Illusion of Safety,* B. J. Packer takes us deep into the unique environment of health and food inspection in a state health department. While that world is foreign to most readers, Packer uses exceptionally well-drawn characters, authentic dialogue, and detailed setting to place us squarely in it.

Murder, gangland intrigue, and hints of romance lead health inspector Laura Nielson and a varied cast of characters on a page-turning adventure. Beginning, quite believably, with a discovery of tainted chicken potpies, the reader is rapidly immersed in ever more dangerous territory in this tightly written drama. The author's clever use of distinctive details in the life of an environmental health specialist heightens the reality of the story while character interaction and crisp, often witty, dialogue aid in driving the tension and complexity toward a harrowing climax.

B. J. Packer's *Illusion of Safety* is certain to entertain and engage—highly recommended reading!

—Duke Southard,
Award-winning author of *The Fallacy of Closure*
and the Detective Parker Havenot series

# ILLUSION
### *of*
# SAFETY

**B. J. PACKER**

*Illusion of Safety*

Published by Wheatmark®
2030 East Speedway Boulevard, Suite 106
Tucson, Arizona 85719 USA
www.wheatmark.com

ISBN: 978-1-62787-992-7 (paperback)
ISBN: 978-1-62787-993-4 (ebook)
LCCN: 2022913572

Bulk ordering discounts are available through Wheatmark, Inc.
For more information, email orders@wheatmark.com or
call 1-888-934-0888.

Disclaimer. This is a work of fiction. Names, characters, places, and events are based solely on the author's imagination and not to be construed as real. Any resemblance to actual persons, living or dead, events, businesses, or locales is entirely coincidental.

# Acknowledgments

Many thanks to the Green Valley Writer's Forum for their comments, suggestions, and encouragement. Special thanks to Duke, Hugh, Larry, Vikki, and Eric for hanging in there with me. Also, thanks to Tom Oehler, BA MT(ASCP), former Public Health Lab Director, City of Minneapolis, for information on lab protocols.

# 1

I just wanted to escape—get out of here, away from the tired hum of cold neon lights, from gray walls, gray floors. My temples throbbed.

Before I could turn off my computer and flee, Jake Schaffner appeared and threw a manila folder on my desk. His usual mischievous grin was missing as he flopped onto an adjacent chair. "Here we go again, Laura. An old guy in ICU. Doesn't sound like he'll make it through the night." He popped open a can of diet cola.

"Another working weekend." I closed my eyes, trying to ignore the pounding in my brain.

"Looks like it," he answered, taking a huge gulp. "It's salmonella again."

Jake and I work for the Minnesota Health Department. I'm an environmental health specialist, known by the more familiar term *health inspector*, and Jake is an epidemiologist investigating the sources of foodborne illness. We often collaborate when an outbreak occurs; Jake interprets data, looking for the precise source of the tainted food, while I inspect the food prep facility, collect food samples, sometimes assist by interviewing ill people, and reinspect. We've had success closing a couple of shoddy operators this year. Sadly, three people died first.

"There'll be litigation, no doubt." I sighed. "How many sick so far?"

"No hard numbers yet," confirmed our director, Franklin Hamilton.

We should have heard him coming. When almost three hundred pounds of solid muscle enters the room, it sucks up a lot of air. Standing nearly six and a half feet, he also does a good job of blocking a doorway. Franklin—never call him Frank—had played pro football for less than a year when he had a career-ending knee injury. Considering all the recent news about Alzheimer's and other brain damage in retired football players, he now thinks the bum knee isn't such a bad deal.

"Here's the Friday night and Saturday game plan." Franklin still uses too many sports analogies for my playbook, but Jake is into it.

Jake threw his hands up in dismay. "This is the second weekend this month we'll be working. The trails are waiting for me, but I can't go. Again." Jake owns a snowmobile and spends most winter weekends in northern Minnesota attacking the trails with his usual enthusiasm. His drama drew no response.

Franklin pulled over one of our flimsy government-issued swivel chairs from another desk and settled his weighty body into the protesting seat. "Laura, I want you to go to Bethany Hospital and get whatever information you can about the ill patient. I'm hoping you'll find some family there. See if the nurses will give you an onset date for his illness."

"Patient privacy laws make that hard to do," I reminded him. "Plus, I don't have your charm."

"Of course you don't." He winked. "But try anyway."

He gave Jake the longer assignment—at least I thought so. "Jake, we have six other complaints that might be related to this salmonella case. By morning, I want a good idea of what food we're looking for. I don't like explaining to families why their loved ones have died from eating dinner."

# 2

Snow had been falling since midafternoon, blowing and swirling and covering my car parked on the ramp's top level. I was just tall enough to clear the car hood and most of the roof with the long-handled snow brush stowed in the trunk since the beginning of November.

With seat heaters on high and defrosters blasting, I gritted my teeth and pulled into traffic, keeping alert for the death-grippers crawling along at fifteen miles per hour and the macho drivers who'd tailgate anybody driving less than the speed limit, regardless of conditions.

I had hoped to make a quick stop at my apartment to feed Dude, the congenial feline who shares my abode. I calculated it would add another thirty or forty minutes under these conditions. He would just have to wait. I would make it up to him with a few extra treats and lap time. Once I merged into a line of traffic, Dude was quickly forgotten.

It took forty-five minutes to drive twelve miles to the hospital. Creep, crawl, stop. Creep, crawl, stop. Normally it took half that time. By the time I reached my destination, exhaustion set in, worsening the already debilitating headache.

Bethany is the primary trauma center in the metro area, and the emergency entrance hums with activity 24/7, especially from 9 p.m. until about 4 a.m. Frequently, city and county cop cars stand near the entrance with lights still flashing.

Not long ago, a shooting happened in the ER waiting room. A gang member decided he preferred his nemesis DOA instead of merely near death. Hospital personnel were safe, but the notoriety lingers.

I left my car in the parking garage across the street and trudged through the five inches already accumulated to get to the visitor's entrance.

The gray-haired receptionist smiled. "May I help you?" Grace settled reading glasses on her nose and readied her hands over the keyboard.

I pulled off my gloves, stuffed them into the pockets of my long down-filled coat, and blew warm breath into my cupped hands before pulling the manila folder out of my briefcase. "Yes, thank you. I'm here to see Art Kruger."

She clicked through her database and looked up, frowning. "He's in ICU. Only family is permitted to visit."

As I showed her my State Health Department ID card, I explained that it was family I wanted to talk with anyway.

Grace stiffened like she was having her own medical emergency. Her face turned the color of gray slushy snow after a few thousand tires have beaten it down. Pressing her hand to her heart, she whispered, "It's not a new, worse variety of COVID, is it?"

Relieved that CPR wouldn't be necessary for Grace, I assured her it definitely was not the deadly virus and then followed her directions—right at the end of the hall, through swinging doors, left down that hall, elevators on the left.

According to the information on the complaint sheet, Art Kruger, eighty-three years old, was admitted to the hospital two days ago with severe dehydration due to vomiting and diarrhea. The hospital lab diagnosed *Salmonella typhimurium* and sent the sample to our state health lab for whole genome sequencing. If the DNA matched that of other salmonella cases in the community or anywhere else in the entire country, then the source of the infection was the same food. Determining what that food might have been was my mission tonight.

It's heartbreaking to meet with the family members of victims who have a serious illness or have died from contaminated food. How do I explain to the parents of an eight-year-old that she died from contaminated salad greens? They purchased the produce expecting it to be healthy and wholesome. What should I say to the family of an elderly woman who died from eating adulterated peanut butter?

What will I say to Art Kruger's family if he dies? First, there will be mourning and then incredible anger. I'm angry too, even more so if the investigations find that contamination was caused by malfeasance.

I approached his room and spotted a middle-aged woman exiting. She walked toward the family waiting area. I assumed she was a member of Art's family and followed her. She was obviously not prepared for our northern climate. Her light-weight—*flimsy* came to mind—white pants and the teal cotton sweater were fine for Florida or California but not for five inches of new snow. Her dark-red polished toenails peeked through the open-weave shoes, and I wondered if she had packed any socks or warm jeans.

"Excuse me. I'm Laura Nielson with Minnesota Public Health. Are you related to Mr. Kruger?" I offered my hand, which she ignored.

"Yes, I'm his daughter Marjorie." She sighed, leaned back in a chair, and closed her eyes. "What do you want?"

This wasn't exactly the start I'd hoped for. "I'm here because, as you're aware, your father has a severe case of salmonella. We think it's very likely it came from contaminated food, so we're trying to determine what he may have eaten in the past week." I took off the now-too-warm coat and hat, letting my hair tumble out to my shoulders. "It's really warm in here," I commented, hoping to melt a little ice. Then I added, "How is he doing?"

She started to cry. "I came as soon as I could." Tears ran from the corners of her reddened eyes and slid down her cheeks. "We talked on Sunday, and he said he wasn't feeling well, had been spending more time on the toilet. That's how he put it. I suggested he see a doctor on Monday. Why didn't I come sooner? He's in a coma now and not going to make it, you know. Now I'll never get to say goodbye." She reached for a hospital tissue from the nearby table.

I squeezed back a few tears of my own before getting down to business. The timing of the illness was important for tracking the contaminated food source. Finding others exposed to the same food was critical. I pulled out the standard questionnaire and asked if she might know if his symptoms started Friday or Saturday of last week.

"He told me he was sick on Friday. That's why I told him

to see a doctor. I told him to drink more water so he didn't get dehydrated, but that's a lost cause. Then he has to pee more often. I suspect he has some prostrate problems and incontinence. Dad wouldn't discuss those issues with me. Thought it was a topic not meant for female ears. I guess you'd say he's old school. He was just so stubborn," she continued. "I wanted him to come to San Diego, at least for the winter months. Get out of this godforsaken cold. How do you stand it?" Not waiting for an answer, she went on. "But he always refused. Said he didn't like my dog. My dog's been dead for three years."

Another tissue.

"He was so inflexible. Same routine every week. Senior center on Monday, poker club on Tuesday, sheepshead game on Thursday." I must have looked confused because she clarified that term. "Sheepshead is a German card game. He never missed it. I worried constantly in the winter that he'd have a driving accident."

I almost hated to interrupt her soul cleansing. "Marjorie, do you think it would be possible to contact his card groups and find out which senior center he attended? It might help me figure out what he ate last week. I'd also like to get samples of food from his refrigerator if you can help with that."

Marjorie sniffed and used another tissue. "I suppose so. One member of his card group is his next-door neighbor, Jim Martin. I don't remember the exact house number, but it's on the north side of Dad's house, if that helps. As far as the refrigerator goes, I'll call you when I get into his house. I expect to be here all night."

After confirming her father's address and giving her my

business card, I picked up my coat and turned to leave Marjorie with her grief. I recognized the devastation, knowing your parent is close to death, already between here and the beyond—the helplessness. When my mother was near the end, her hospice nurse offered compassionate advice: *Tell her you love her and wish her a peaceful journey. She will hear you.*

I turned back and put a hand on Marjorie's shoulder. "Hold his hand, say goodbye. He'll know you're here."

# 3

It was still snowing, my headache lingered, and I was not eager to get back on the icy streets. The newspaper headlines and TV weather announcers had predicted the first polar vortex of the winter, a new term for the same old thing: bitter cold. Passing the hospital cafeteria on my way out, I figured a warm coffee was a preferable option to a cold car.

I asked for a glass of water with the coffee and drank it down with two migraine tablets before taking the hot beverage and heading to the dining area.

"Laura," he called from a table in the corner. "What brings you here?" Detective Thomas Garcia had been the lead officer for a hostage negotiation in a restaurant a couple of months ago. It was my misfortune to have been in the building during the standoff. That's how we met. We've had coffee a few times since, and we've tried to go out twice, both times interrupted and ending when his phone rang.

Thomas has dark brown eyes that seem to see what you're thinking, which I suppose is a good trait for a cop. He's not particularly tall, probably around five ten, but it looks as if he's all muscle. Not bulky, just very firm and unyielding. His dynamite smile melted my wariness, which is probably also good for a cop. Potentially, I suppose we're compatible, but I still carry some tattered baggage from a brief nasty marriage six years ago. Very heavy, very battered baggage.

"Everything okay?"

"Following up on a case of salmonella. An elderly man in ICU probably isn't going to make it." I pulled out the opposite chair and set my coffee on the yellow tabletop. Designers must use colors like this to cheer people up, but under fluorescent lights, the tables were the shade of fresh phlegm. "What about you? You're not just hanging around the hospital trying to pick up a date on Friday night."

He grinned at my smart-ass comment but followed with a grimace. "Another homicide. At first, they thought the guy was either a drunk or another overdose, but when the patrol guys turned him over, the body was bloody. He was shot a couple times. They found him in the alley behind one of the stores on Fourteenth Avenue. Familiar with Javier's Meats?"

"Oh, yeah, I know it. Javier was caught selling uninspected meat twice in two months. Department of Agriculture inspectors are having a hearing with him next week."

"Don't think so," Thomas replied. "Javier is dead." Planting his elbows on the table, he rested his chin on his fists. "And what specifics might you have about Javier that I need to know?"

"It started last month with a foodborne illness complaint inspection. When I showed him the complaint, he was quite vociferous, arguing there was no possible way anybody could have gotten ill from meat. I'm used to hearing denials—that's par for the course—but he was nasty and tried to push me out the door. After I threatened to call the police, he let me inspect, followed my every step, and declared he had lost the key for his meat cooler. Honestly, Thomas, nobody ever locks walk-in coolers. I suspected he had something in that cooler besides meat, so I suggested none too politely that he'd better find the key before the next day, or we'd get a search warrant.

"So," I continued to explain, "when the meat inspectors from State Ag descended upon him the next morning—three of them, to be exact—Javier had miraculously found his key, and the cooler was unlocked. Only one pig carcass was hanging in there; it didn't have an inspection stamp, and Ag cited him."

"You said this happened twice." Thomas finished his coffee.

"Yeah. Ag walked in on him early one morning last week before business hours and found eight carcasses hanging there without inspection stamps, including a couple of pigs that didn't look at all wholesome. That's when they embargoed the meat and set the hearing date. They required him to bring all his purchase and sales records for the last three months. Javier threatened the inspector. Ag planned to have a security officer at the hearing." My coffee was still too hot. I blew over the surface.

"What exactly does the embargo do?"

"It prohibits him from selling the meat. Ag and Javier were discussing terms to destroy the product. Javier hadn't agreed to everything yet."

Thomas asked a few more questions, including the name of the Ag inspector whom Javier had threatened. "I'm glad you're no longer involved in this. I'd be worried," he admitted. "Have you considered carrying a gun?"

"Are you crazy?" I blurted, almost choking on a mouthful of hot liquid. "I can't carry a gun in my work."

"You don't think the murder of Javier outside a place you just inspected in a neighborhood where gangs operate isn't worrisome?"

Damn those dark eyes. He was looking straight into my indignant green ones, waiting for me to blink. I did. "Javier's death has absolutely nothing to do with my work, Thomas. And you know Franklin wouldn't approve of a concealed weapon."

"I'm not so sure about that," he mused.

"Well, I definitely am. Gotta go." I shoved away from the table.

# 4

The night was getting colder. The snow had stopped, and the sky was clearing from the northwest. It meant we could expect a frigid night, close to zero. November was too soon in the winter season for temperatures so low, but it was Minnesota, after all. The fact that official winter didn't come for another month made no difference in the land of the frozen tundra.

I found Art Kruger's house in an older part of the city where neat little bungalows from the 1930s lined the streets. The neighborhood had not yet been overwhelmed by the trend to tear down the small, cozy homes and erect megahouses a foot from each lot line. Lights were on next door in the Martin house, and someone was bent over, shoveling the front sidewalk.

I grabbed my briefcase and my small sample cooler and slammed the car door to alert the shoveler that someone was nearby. An older woman was hunched over the shovel, wearing a wool jacket too thin to keep her warm.

"Excuse me, I'm looking for Jim Martin. Is this his house?"

She tried to stand up straight. "Who are you, and what do

you want?" She kept her distance and made no effort to move toward me or the house.

I showed her my ID and explained about her neighbor in the hospital. "I've been told Mr. Kruger played cards with Jim Martin. What I'm hoping is that Mr. Martin can remember what they ate last week at their card game and provide contact information for the other players. It will help us determine what specific food made Mr. Kruger so ill."

"Jim's in there, and he's sick too. Been that way for a couple of days. Maybe he has the same thing. He's always complaining about something or another, so I hardly listen anymore. I suppose you want to talk to him?"

"Yes. If you think he's able, I'd appreciate a few minutes of his time."

She trudged up the sidewalk, opened the door, and nodded for me to follow.

Stepping through the front door was like walking into a sauna. It felt like eighty degrees in the house, and the odor of unwashed bodies, vomit, and diarrhea was seeping into every waft of air. I closed my eyes for a few seconds to visualize blooming roses and peonies. It didn't help much, but for the time being, my stomach stopped rebelling.

She removed her coat and hat and introduced herself. "I'm Dorothy Martin. Throw your coat on that chair. He's in here," she said, leading me into the living room.

Jim Martin was watching a giant TV in a small living room dominated by his torso in an oversized leather recliner. Next to it sat a tired and threadbare upholstered rocker.

He didn't look away from the screen when his wife introduced me. His bulging bare stomach poked out over his pajama pants, and the flannel top was soiled from vomit. Appearing pale and listless, Jim still managed to bark at me, or possibly his wife, "What the hell do you want?"

He perked up a little when told about Art Kruger's hospitalization for foodborne illness. I asked him if he had shared any food with his neighbor in the past week. "How's Art doing?" he replied, ignoring my request.

"He's in ICU, and his daughter Marjorie is with him."

"Marjorie? Really? Been a long time since she's been home," Dorothy commented. "They didn't get along that well. Art always said he didn't like her lifestyle. Not sure why." She leaned against the wall. "I'd have spent winter in San Diego any time she asked me."

"Bah, she lives with another woman, that's why, you stupid cow," Jim ranted before vomiting into a big red plastic bowl. He used a grubby-looking towel to wipe his mouth and scruffy facial hair before tossing it at his wife.

"Get me a clean one," he ordered.

I wanted to clobber him right between the eyes. Instead, I stepped closer and looked at his color and then pinched the back of his hand to get an indication of dehydration. His skin was burning to the touch. He glared at me and jerked his hand away.

"Mrs. Martin, I think you should take your husband to the emergency room. He appears to be severely dehydrated and running a high fever."

"Stupid woman isn't driving me anywhere," Jim Martin bellowed. "She's a lousy driver." With all his energy spent in the outburst, he sank further into the recliner.

She sighed and sat down in her ratty chair. "He won't let

me drive him anywhere. The phone's over there." She pointed to an end table next to the sofa. "You can call nine-one-one." I did.

While we waited for the EMTs, I inquired about her health and if she knew of any foods Jim may have shared with Art Kruger in the past week. Dorothy replied that the two men were part of a card group that met every Thursday, except yesterday it had been canceled because Art was sick and Jim wasn't feeling great either. I asked about the health of others in the group. She didn't talk to them. She didn't know.

The emergency technicians arrived and, after evaluating Jim Martin, loaded him into the back of the waiting ambulance for transport. They asked Dorothy if she wanted to ride along, but she declined. "I'll come later," she mumbled.

With Dorothy's approval, I bagged, labeled, and documented several foods stored in her refrigerator, including some bologna and a lone hot dog.

I was ready to leave and found her still on the rocker, swaying back and forth, staring at the carpet. I put on my coat. "I'm going now, Dorothy. Is there someone I can call for you?" She ignored me.

The shovel was standing next to the front door, not even half of the snow removed from the sidewalk. Ten minutes later, I had cleared it to concrete.

The drive back to the Health Department was much quicker and less hazardous. An army of snowplows had cleared the freeway. The death-grippers were snug in their homes, and the macho drivers were still at the bars—it was, after all, Friday night. The roads would get dangerous again around midnight, long after I was home.

I stopped in the office to see how Jake was progressing. He was hunched over his computer, mumbling. I plunked the small cooler on a nearby desk, removed my gloves, and unzipped my coat.

"Someone still in the lab?"

"Yeah, a tech is there setting up plates," he confirmed.

"Find something possible?"

"Maybe something in this cooler. What about you? Having any luck contacting people?"

"Nothing of significance yet," he replied without looking away from the screen.

I threw my coat on a chair and pulled off the fur-lined Sorrel boots, opting to go to the lab in my wool socks.

"Be back in five, and by the way," I added just before closing the door, "the cops found the owner of Javier's Meats dead behind his store tonight. Remember him? He's the guy Ag is after for uninspected meat."

Jake had the small office television turned on for the nine o'clock news when I returned, which was closer to fifteen minutes than five. "How'd you find out about Javier so soon?"

I hesitated telling Jake the truth. Something about the hostage situation, and Thomas in particular, was a burr in his lab plate. He never acknowledged what it was, but his contempt was obvious whenever I mentioned this particular cop.

"Ran into Thomas at the hospital. He's on this case."

Before Jake could come up with a snarky comment about the coincidence, the reporter appeared on the screen to describe a murder behind the market. While not confirming the identity of the dead man, she related that the owner had been under investigation by the State Department of

Agriculture for selling unsafe meat. She then referred customers to the state foodborne illness hotline in case anyone thought they had become ill from eating any product from the market.

"Free publicity. That'll keep you busy tomorrow," I said. His phone rang. "And maybe tonight too. See you in the morning. I'm going home. I'm hungry."

"Wait," he said before taking the call. "I could let this go to voicemail. Want to stop for a burger and a beer?"

"No, thanks. It's late. My head aches. I want to get home. Got a waiting cat to feed."

# 5

My phone rang before eight on Saturday morning. I jolted upright and reached for the cell. Caller ID identified him. "Thomas, this better be good because I'm not done sleeping."

"Sorry, Laura, but I need your help."

"This early? You've got to be kidding. Don't you have the weekend off or something?" Dude, my fourteen-pound tom-cat, was already annoyed with the disturbance and expressed his displeasure with a growl of disgust.

"I'll pick up a skinny mocha with a chocolate swirl and meet you at Javier's in forty-five minutes." He knew my weakness.

"I assume this is important, very important, Detective." I threw off the blankets and reached for my robe.

"Yes, it's important. And give my regards to the Dude," he added before ending the call.

Sometimes I think Thomas pulls the good cop/bad cop stuff on me. This morning, he was all business and a little curt. But when saying hello to my cat, he's more empathetic and relaxed. That's been the case during our two dinners together.

We laugh and relax, and then his phone rings, and he's out the door. One time he'd forgotten he'd picked me up, and I had to take a cab home—no apologies from him either.

Forty-five minutes later, I pulled into the parking lot behind Javier's Market. My hair was still damp, so I kept the Minnesota Vikings knit cap pulled down over my ears and eyebrows. Thomas met me at the back door, handed me the latte, and pulled off the stocking cap. It was a little bit playful and something unexpected. I took a sip of the java and lifted my eyebrows in question.

"First, I apologize for calling early."

I must have looked surprised because he gave me a broad smile and a quick nod.

"I want you to walk through the store and point out anything that doesn't appear normal for a meat market. Since you were here recently, you might remember if anything has changed."

Javier's was a typical ethnic meat market serving a growing immigrant population as well as locals. The deli case featured bowls of salads, and he sold sub sandwiches. He and his staff made several different varieties of sausage sold fresh from the front display case. His beer and chorizo sausages had an excellent review in the "Taste" section of the *Star Tribune* last year, which created a huge boost in his sales. Clients were driving in from the suburbs for his products. Wholesale business boomed.

Thomas removed the yellow tape and opened the back door. The smell of unrefrigerated meat and poultry almost choked us.

"Was the heat turned up? Who's been in here?" I sniffed my latte to mask the stench. "Did you guys turn off the meat cases? Or is there another body in here?"

"We," he emphasized the word, "didn't do anything." He led me to an uncovered blue plastic waste barrel next to the meat-cutting table. Chunks of skin and bones that had once belonged to a pig, chicken feet still attached to yellow scaly legs, and other unidentifiable scraps were covered with slime. "This is how it was last night when the lab techs were in here. They wondered the same thing."

"This," I said, pointing at the barrel while holding my nose, "has been here longer than overnight. And it better go in the cooler to prevent maggot growth. It's not going to be pretty here in another day or two." I propped open the back door to let the sharp cold cut through the stench.

"We already have photos." Thomas reached for the barrel.

"Take off your coat so you don't get slop in it because it will reek for days." He handed his camel-colored parka to me before rolling the barrel toward the cooler. I opened the heavy door and was surprised. "Was this empty last night? Javier was supposed to be working with Ag on disposition of the embargoed carcasses, but it usually doesn't happen this quickly."

"Could they have been stolen? There were tire tracks in the snow backed up to the door. Looks like a smaller truck, probably some kind of van."

"I suppose someone could steal meat to resell in spite of the condemnation tags, but they'd have to sell it darn fast before it starts smelling as bad as the blue barrel. Those carcasses were already over two weeks old."

"Look around some more and tell me what you see. Is it usual to have all these boxes of chemicals stacked here?" Thomas pointed to a stack of eight cases near the back door.

"Looks like they were delivered recently and nobody put them away yet." I took another deep sniff of coffee aroma.

"How recently? What would be normal?"

"Depends how busy they were and how badly they needed it." I inspected the boxes. "Pilot Chemical Company. These top four boxes are gallons of sanitizer; bottom six are detergent."

"They need that much, huh?"

"Yes, Thomas, they use plenty. This is enough for two to three months. Maybe he got a bulk discount."

"A detail I needed to understand. What else can you tell me?"

First, I noted that the saw table had not been cleaned, something I knew Javier would not have left in that condition. There were little scraps of meat on the cutting table and crusty blood pools on the floor. I wondered if he'd been interrupted while working.

"Have you talked to any of his employees? They must know something about all of this..." I stopped, searching for an appropriate descriptive term. "This bloody mess."

"We're trying to locate them now. We think at least one of them was illegal, and if so, he'll skip town once he hears about the murder."

Thomas handed me a box of small zip-lock bags. "What would a meat market use this size bag for?"

"Maybe individual portions of dry spice mixes. I don't know. There might be several reasons. Why?"

"Just curious."

The meat market office shocked me. Javier had been meticulous about his records. In fact, I always thought he was a little paranoid about them. Two weeks ago when we reviewed his temperature charts and employee illness logs, Javier had to unlock the file drawer to retrieve them. That's pretty standard information in the food business. I couldn't think of any reason for this security.

The office had been ransacked: File cabinet drawers pulled out and the contents strewn on the floor. Desk drawers left open in disarray. "He was supposed to hand over purchase records at the hearing next week. We still want to find the supplier of the meat."

"Expand your thinking about those records," Thomas suggested. "What would be the very worst penalty for Javier or the meat supplier if the carcasses weren't inspected?"

"Since it's the second violation for uninspected meat, he'd get a heavy fine and oversight for at least a year. The task of finding the suppliers—I suspect they don't have any legal license or location—would go to either State Ag or USDA. The processor would be closed down."

"So in your opinion, it's not serious enough to commit murder?"

"No, Thomas, it doesn't make sense at all." As I knelt to gather papers from the floor, he handed me latex gloves.

"These documents are being collected this morning. Very soon." He gave a knowing look, and I pulled on the gloves before sorting through the piles. "The copy machine is in the corner. I'll be up front when you're finished." The door closed.

In less than a half hour, I'd managed to copy and begin

sorting the invoices into loosely stacked piles, one for paper products and dry goods like spices, herbs, and salts; another for chemicals and pest control services; a pile for repairs and garbage removal; and the last one for receipts and supplier invoices for meats. I'd also found Javier's food safety records that we'd reviewed during my inspection two weeks ago. What was missing were his records from the past week. Javier had been required to bring these records and the invoices to his hearing.

"Thomas," I opened the office door and yelled, "look for a thin black three-ring binder with the letters H-A-C-C-P on the cover. It should be in the processing area somewhere." I left the door open. The small room was stuffy with a flowery odor of either cheap perfume or nasty aftershave that was giving me a headache even the coffee couldn't conquer. Stuffing the copied records into my oversized purse, I went back to the processing area and found Thomas holding the black ring binder.

He was looking through the pages when we heard car doors slamming behind the building. The other investigators had arrived. I took the book from Thomas and stuffed it in my now-bulging bag.

"Get it back to me tonight," he ordered.

I nodded. "I need to get to the office. They're expecting me."

"I see I'm not the only one who works on weekends." He was grinning when I left.

# 6

Four student interns were working the phones when I arrived at the office. Last night's news about the murder behind the market and Javier's uninspected meat made the first page of the *Star Tribune's* "Minnesota" section, and it produced a new record for calls to the Health Department on a Saturday morning. The interns were completing questionnaires and handing Jake the information to evaluate. For some who called, it was the vicarious thrill of having shopped in the market as long ago as September. One caller wanted to know what time the murder happened because maybe he'd seen the perpetrator about three o'clock yesterday afternoon. He was advised to call the police.

Before I could even take off my coat, Jake's face, bright blue eyes, and familiar smile appeared above the six-foot partition. "Do you have any contacts from that Kruger guy for follow-up? So far the calls we're getting don't appear to be related to this salmonella case or to the previous illness from Javier's."

After I pulled the copies of meat market invoices and the black binder out of my purse and stacked them on my desk, I opened my briefcase to find the contact information Dorothy Martin had given me. Jake paged through the copied information.

"Where did you get this?"

"From Javier's."

"Today? Isn't the place sealed off by the police?"

"Kind of." I kept my head down, pretending to look for the information he wanted.

It was deathly quiet for ten seconds while he sifted through the photocopies.

"Don't let Franklin know how you got these, or it could be big trouble."

"Thomas permitted me to copy all of it," I replied with a little more defiance than was necessary.

"That guy's going to get you into trouble if you're not careful," he admonished and then left, all huffy and out of sorts. At least that was my impression of his somewhat childish reaction as soon as he knew Thomas was involved.

Before I could stuff those papers into Javier's file, the phone rang.

"Laura, this is Marjorie Kruger, Art's daughter. My father died early this morning. I'm at his house now. Can you come and clean out the refrigerator?"

I offered my sympathies and agreed to be there in thirty minutes. Cleaning out a refrigerator wasn't what I had in mind for the morning, but it would be good to get more samples for the lab. Plus, I figured it would be helpful for Marjorie to have someone to talk to while she was dealing with memories in her dead father's house.

Franklin was leaving the lab as I entered to pick up a

cooler and the chain of custody paperwork. "I'm assuming you know about Javier."

"Yes, I saw Thomas at the hospital last night after talking to Mr. Kruger's daughter. He told me."

"Okay, so there'll be no administrative hearing next week. I'll cancel the room."

"We have another problem," I replied. "This morning, Thomas called me to walk through the market with him to see what might be out of place or unusual. All the embargoed meat was gone."

Franklin shook his head. "I'll contact Ag and public relations for media coverage and reserve a larger meeting room."

# 7

Marjorie answered the door wearing a T-shirt and shorts. I must have shown surprise because, before I could say a word, she blurted, "I know, I know. I should have brought warmer clothes. I just turned up the heat, so throw your coat on the sofa. It's the only clear space in the house."

She was right on that assessment. Neat piles of the daily newspaper leaned against the walls of the small entry. Magazine stacks four feet high and three issues wide of *National Geographic, Time, Reader's Digest,* and other publications appeared to support a wall, and more magazines were piled on the dining room table, daring the formal furniture to host a meal. A collection of beautiful cut glass in various sizes and colors sat on the coffee table and end tables in the living room and inside a lighted curio cabinet. I guessed they were worth several thousand dollars. Every piece was dust-free and sparkling.

"He was a saver but very neat," Marjorie explained. "Couldn't bear to throw out anything that might have another use. I didn't realize the crystal collection had grown so large.

He must have ordered most of those after Mother died. It's been twelve years."

"What are you going to do?" I swept my arms around in question. She held her hands in a the-heck-if-I-know pose as I walked into the kitchen, not sure what to expect. Piles of washed black plastic containers, common with so many frozen convenience foods, sat on the counters. More magazines occupied a corner behind the small glass-top breakfast table.

I opened the refrigerator door and discovered some deli chicken and macaroni salad with recent use-by dates and leftover something in another one of those black plastic bowls. I documented all the temperatures with my thermometer, dated and documented the time everything was sampled, including the mystery product, and sealed the sample bags while Marjorie was still rummaging through cupboards, pulling out boxes and cans.

"Will the food pantry take any of these?"

"Depends on the expiration date. They don't want things past the date because the clients think the food is old and not safe. This isn't factual, but it's what happens, so people throw out decent food."

"Thanks. I'll check them all and chuck the old stuff."

"Do you know who your father's other card-playing friends are? It's important we contact them for follow-up as soon as possible. Which senior center did he attend?"

She shuffled through papers on the counter, found a yellow sticky note, and handed it to me. "Here are the names and phone numbers of his old 'Nam buddies. They got together nearly every week. I'll start looking through his phone lists this afternoon and call you with other names and the senior center."

"It'd be faster if you called the foodborne illness hotline." I stuffed her small bit of information into my briefcase and extracted a card with the number. "The epidemiology staff will take the info and make the contacts right away."

Although I had these altruistic plans to continue helping Marjorie, my watch indicated otherwise. I gave her some contacts for possible help cleaning out the house, grabbed my things, and left.

I stored the cooler in the car trunk and walked next door to see how Dorothy Martin was doing. She answered the door immediately, almost as if she'd been watching from the window.

"How is your husband?"

"He's still breathing."

"Do you have somewhere safe to go, a child's house or a good friend? You don't have to stay here."

"Too many years to change things now. It is what it is."

"There are resources, Dorothy, other options." I gave her a card for the Minnesota Domestic Abuse resources. "Call them if you want more information. They'll help you."

She took the card, shoved it in her pocket, and slammed the door in my face. A whiff of stale air found merciful escape, fleeing into the cold, crisp morning, gaining new life.

Either the odious smell of rotting meat in Javier's or the foul air whooshing out of the Martin house had triggered another miserable headache. Maybe both. Sometimes it's a curse to have a discriminating olfactory ability. I often wondered why a dog doesn't get sick from continually picking up scents. A dog has two hundred twenty million olfactory receptors enabling it to walk into a room with thirty people sitting around and determine that number thirty-one is hiding in the closet. And it wags its tail happily the entire time. A human has only five million receptors, and most of us can't distinguish who's drowning in Chanel or who has slapped on Armani.

All my receptors work overtime. I can walk into a kitchen and smell cockroaches, which is a pretty disgusting ability. Old grease in the deep-fat fryers? Yep, smell that too. And mold and sewer gas in a basement. Some places smell awesome, like the French bakery or a restaurant that uses olive oil and fresh rosemary. For many other odors, migraine pills get me through the day.

At a coffee drive-thru, the barista handed me a large coffee cooler, no whip, which is ridiculous when there is snow on the ground and the overnight low was near zero. The pills don't go down easily with hot drinks, so I held the plastic cup with gloved hands and took a deep breath of the fresh winter landscape.

The office was quiet when I returned. According to the two interns still waiting to answer phones, Jake had already left for the day as calls from the public had yielded little useful information thus far. There would be additional news on the front page of the Sunday paper alerting the public about the stolen meat carcasses, plus a live interview with the commissioner of health on the evening television broadcasts.

I rang the two card-playing friends of Art Kruger and left messages asking them to return my call. Art's death from salmonella weighed on my mind. If these other men who played cards with him were in fragile health, they were also at great risk. Maybe they were already in the hospital. There was nothing to be done but wait.

# 8

Dude had been purring since I arrived home. I wasn't sure if it was me he was happy to see or if it was the grocery bag with his favorite food. I felt guilty about leaving him alone on a Saturday and gave him the full can of chicken in gravy. He snarfed it up and rubbed my legs in satisfaction.

"There's no way you're getting any more. And you better not vomit on the bed either," I advised as if he understood.

The Dude is a fine specimen of a tomcat with silky gray fur, broad shoulders, and a confident strut. His striking blue eyes miss nothing, and his satisfied purring is a great comfort at the end of the day. He always listens with great understanding unless it's time to eat or time to sleep or time to just plain ignore me.

He soon figured out there wouldn't be any more attention coming his way, so he sauntered into the living room and curled up on the sofa. I started preparing my dinner.

The phone rang when my salmon was sizzling under the oven broiler, about one minute left to perfection. It was Thomas.

"Can you call back in thirty minutes?" I pleaded.

"Want to go out for dinner, or should I bring carryout?"

"Really, Thomas? An invitation at this hour? My fish is nearly finished. If it overcooks, it'll be very expensive cat food."

"I'll bring spring rolls and phô, and we can have it with the fish. How does that sound?" He paused. "Or you can eat your food, and I'll just bring enough for one."

"What's this sudden need to talk on a Saturday night? Don't you have to work or something?" I turned on the speakerphone and pulled the fillet out of the oven. It looked wonderful, but if I waited for Thomas to arrive, it would no longer be hot. And did I even want to wait for him?

"What's the deal?" I was irritated at his assumptions— first, that I wasn't busy on a Saturday night and, second, that I would just drop everything when he called. Plus, I was wary. I hadn't invited another man into my apartment since the divorce. Thomas was inviting himself.

"I do need the black binder back, as you may recall. And we searched Javier's house today. Are you interested or not?" He sounded a bit testy.

"Should I be?"

"I think so, yes."

"How long before you get here?" The salmon could go in a salad tomorrow.

"Ten to fifteen minutes."

The entrance buzzer rang eight minutes later. It was obvious he already had the takeout food and had parked the car nearby when he called.

"That was fast," I commented. "Almost too fast, don't you think, Detective?"

He grinned. "Good deduction. I was hoping you hadn't eaten yet."

"What would you have done if I said I wanted pizza?"

"Redirected the conversation until you forgot about pizza." The tension broke.

The food came from my favorite Asian restaurant. The spring rolls, wrapped in rice paper and stuffed with thin slices of barbecued pork, tender shrimp, fresh cucumber, thin rice noodles, and cilantro, came with a tasty peanut sauce. The phô, a soup with seasoned chicken stock, shrimp, rice noodles, calamari, and fish balls, was still steaming when I divided it into two bowls.

"How did you know this is my favorite restaurant?"

"A good cop knows everything."

"Sounds like spying to me." I tried to sound upset, but it wasn't working. After we finished slurping broth and noodles, Dude hopped on his lap and started to purr. "Fickle cat," I admonished when he rubbed his head against Thomas's chest. Dude didn't like most men. He usually retreated to the bedroom when I had guests. This affinity for Thomas both amazed and irritated me. Dude and I would have a conversation about this later tonight, and he would either ignore me or purr understandingly.

Thomas put the cat on the floor and started to clear the dishes. We spent a few silent moments cleaning the counters and loading the soiled items into the dishwasher and then moved into my small living room, where Mozart was playing from the iPod speaker. The classical composer's music often helped ease the tension of my migraines. Thomas sat on the sofa, and I took the wing chair. The traitor cat curled up next to Thomas and started purring again.

"Nice music," he commented in a small-talk way of opening a conversation.

"Wolfgang Amadeus," I answered, glaring at the Dude.

"Ah, Mozart." He smiled like he'd just won a contest to identify the composer. "I like it. It's soothing."

Well, crap, how could I stay upset? He'd brought my favorite takeout food, helped clean up the kitchen, liked Mozart, and indulged the cat. He appeared to be a really decent guy, and since he was a cop, I expected him to be safe.

"Tell me about Javier's house, Thomas. I'm curious why you think I should know about it right away."

He related that Friday night after Javier's body was found and taken to the morgue, a detective went to his house to inform his family. The house was dark when he arrived. Nobody responded to the doorbell. What was most surprising was its location in an expensive area of southwest Minneapolis, which raised immediate suspicions. It didn't seem probable the owner of a small business in the central city could afford such an expensive house in that upscale neighborhood.

"This morning while some investigators boxed up evidence at the meat market, others proceeded to Javier's house with a search warrant. No one was home, and they forced a side door. Since Javier's cell phone hadn't been found on his body or in the market, and the business computer was missing, the investigators were hoping there was another computer at the house.

"The house had been torn apart, especially the home office," Thomas explained. "They found other rooms trashed as well. Bed mattresses overturned, opened drawers dumped on the floor, even floorboards pulled up in a bedroom. The investigators think the intruders were looking for drugs."

"Oh, not Javier." I sighed. "I thought he was one of the good guys. What about his wife and son? Are they okay? He was so proud of his son."

"We don't know where they are. If there had been physical violence in the house, there should have been blood. There wasn't any. The investigators contacted cell phone companies looking for a second phone number that might lead them to survivors. They're checking the airlines for reservations in any of their names. At this point, it's all they can do."

"Whenever I inspected the meat market, Javier walked along with me, and sometimes we did get off the subject," I confessed. "Once, he told me about growing up in a southern California barrio and how his entire family struggled to get by. He told me how moving to Minnesota had been a step up. His son had an American first name, attended a good school, and had a much better life."

"What I'd like you to do," Thomas said, interrupting my musing, "is to look at the paperwork you copied for unusual expenses or something that doesn't fit with a meat market."

"Thomas, I don't know much about the day-to-day operation of a meat market. Other than the food-safety aspect, I have no idea what to look for."

"You'll know it when you find it," he encouraged. "Trust me."

Those two words struck me like the lies and fury behind a violent drunk who loses control. I wanted to scream, "You're not trustworthy!" Instead, I swallowed the bitter lump in my throat, willed my hands not to shake, and asked Thomas to leave. "I'll look carefully at the records and let you know if something looks out of place."

Rising from the chair, I moved to the door, bidding him goodnight. His perplexed look didn't surprise me. He picked up his jacket and closed the door without saying goodbye. He'd forgotten the black ring binder.

I spent the rest of the night and all day Sunday analyzing and reanalyzing my reaction, trying to devise a better strategy to cope with ugly flashbacks. And thinking about an apology.

# 9

On Sunday morning, the local television stations and the *Minneapolis Star Tribune* and *St. Paul Press* carried the story about the stolen meat. The reporter implied the carcasses may have been cut up and redistributed to other ethnic meat markets. By Sunday evening, the Latino community announced a march to protest this discrimination, and mayors in both cities scheduled meetings with the leaders and the paper editors early the next afternoon.

When I arrived Monday morning, office phones were rattling, and local news was airing on the office TV. I found Jake bent over his computer, two empty diet cola cans on his desk. The lab had printed the DNA profile for Art Kruger's salmonella, and he was looking for the same alignment of bars and spaces from other similar illnesses on the national database maintained by the Centers for Disease Control and Prevention (CDC).

"Good Sunday?"

He looked up and grinned, exposing his sunburned nose. "Snow was pretty good yesterday. Used the trails in Itasca

County. Lakes aren't frozen yet, but if we get the usual cold and snow at Thanksgiving, it should be good for the winter."

"Too early for all this snow," Franklin predicted as he put another manila folder on Jake's desk. "It'll all melt next week, and you'll have to wait for January for another good storm."

"What are you, the extra-perceptive weather forecaster of the Twin Cities?" I shook my head with a smile. "Or is it just wishful thinking?"

"Little bit of both," he admitted. "The Gophers play their last home football game on Saturday. I'd prefer not to shovel snow from my seat. Plus," he winked, "the long-range forecast predicts less precipitation than normal for the next six weeks."

"Well, that ices it then." Jake smirked. "We know these forecasts are always, always right on." He paused for effect. "Don't think I'll put my machine in storage just yet."

Verbal sparring over the weather was a ritualized pastime for these two. Jake thrived on outdoor sports. He made an exaggerated effort of complaining when weekend work interfered with these leisure pursuits, and Franklin took delight in providing weather reports that countered Jake's expectations. It wasn't that Franklin didn't enjoy the seasons; he fished year round. He just liked giving Jake a hard time. And he didn't mind snow—just not on his stadium seat.

"Any more on the Art Kruger case?" Franklin turned and looked at me.

"His daughter called in contact information on Saturday. The interns are on it. I'll call the other two guys in his card club again today and also check on Jim Martin. Did the hospital send his stool sample over yet?" I thought again of Dorothy. Maybe her husband would die and free her, but then what?

"In the lab as we speak." Jake interrupted my wandering thoughts.

"We have the large conference room reserved for the meeting with State Ag," Franklin announced. "We have a new agenda. Foremost, the source of those carcasses."

"There must be some record of delivery and payment," I added, "though it might be disguised as another supplier. This is just the beginning of a very long traceback and verification for Ag and USDA. And Thomas suggested we look for anything unusual in the receipts."

"And what does Thomas think you'll discover?" Jake snapped.

Franklin looked at Jake and then at me, sensing a different current in the air. "Weelll," he said, dragging out the word to two syllables, buying time to compose his thoughts. "I'd guess Thomas knows his business, just like you know yours. If he thinks Laura and the inspectors from Ag might come upon suspect documents, he's probably correct. Wouldn't you agree, Jake?"

Jake answered with a clipped "yeah" and went back to his computer.

# 10

We had the paperwork from Javier's stacked into six categories: invoices for meat and other food products, invoices for nonfood items, special-order sales receipts, general market sales, the daily logs for the food-safety plan, and the employee work schedules. I wasn't sure why Darren wanted it organized this way, but he'd insisted, and when he glared over his wire-rimmed glasses, nobody disagreed.

Darren Wolfe has done a heck of a lot more tracebacks than I have, and I wasn't about to question his method. He has supervised the state meat inspectors for fifteen years. We'd worked with him before, following the trail of ground beef that caused an *E. coli* outbreak and the source of jalapeño peppers that were contaminated with *Salmonella Saintpaul*. His colleagues described him as rough around the edges, single-minded, and unyielding. Rumor had it his direct reports couldn't wait until Darren retired.

I contributed copies of the most recent records I had copied in Javier's ransacked office. Darren gave me a pile of delivery receipts Javier had given Ag before his death. He wanted each supplier verified.

Inspectors are familiar with the main players for food distribution in the Twin Cities. We share information. We know who's reliable and who could improve. But when it comes to out-of-state suppliers, especially smaller businesses with limited clients, we need to verify their license information, including transport truck licensing, and we request a copy of their most recent inspection.

Traceback charts can get messy, with arrows following the flow of product like snake tracks in the sand. As I looked at these records, I saw reptiles swerving.

"Ever hear of Ricardo's Fresh Meats?" I asked no one in particular.

Darren and the two other inspectors stopped and looked at me and then at each other. "Ah, damn, here we go again. What's the business address? I'll get on this one right away."

"Interesting thing about these receipts," I continued, paging through the stack. "There are only three from Ricardo's, and those were found in Javier's office Saturday morning after he was murdered. There aren't any other receipts for Ricardo's. Is it possible Javier manufactured different receipts for his hearing?"

"Would he be stupid enough to not realize we'd ask about them?" Darren answered his own question. "Nah, he was crafty. He'd know better. But check it out anyway." He shuffled through more papers. "See if we can come close to reconciling the net weight of the products received with the pounds of product sold."

"Huh?" I shook my head.

"What comes in must go somewhere. We need to figure out what net weight comes in first. If the meat market received hog carcasses at a specific weight, we have charts to tell us how many pounds of finished product can come from it, including different cuts, trim, back fat, and bacon. So we look at his invoices and his sales and reconcile."

"You want this done again?" complained one Ag inspector. "It's going to take a lot of hours. And we're not sure we have all his records."

Darren took off his glasses and glared. "Look, guys and gals," he nodded toward me and the other woman from Ag, "we've got an unknown number of uninspected hog carcasses out there, we've got an unknown source for them, plus a murdered man who may be in that state due to these carcasses." He put his glasses back on and gave us assignments.

# 11

Our meeting ended at noon. We paged through invoices and found huge gaps in dates, and I wondered if Javier had thrown some of his paperwork in the dumpster. But wouldn't he have shredded it? I didn't recall a shredder in his office. Thomas would certainly know if the investigators had pulled documents from the garbage. I left a message and returned to monitor my own voicemail.

The first call came from Janet Larson, wife of Oscar. Yes, her husband played cards with Art Kruger and Jim Martin. No, he wasn't sick. No, she didn't think we needed to interview him. His memory wasn't very good. Click. Message two was from the fourth card player. Yes, he had a little diarrhea last week but was over it.

I wanted to talk to both of those men and find out what they did and did not eat. Caller number two with the slight diarrhea turned out to be Peter Born, who, like the other card players, was in his late seventies but apparently in a much healthier condition than Art or Jim. At least that was his take on it. And, sure, he'd be glad to complete an interview. He'd hosted the card party, and I could sample anything in his refrigerator I wanted. How soon would I be there?

I had no desire to continue shuffling through Javier's invoices. Instead, I picked up gear from the lab, programmed the address into the cell phone GPS, and headed out.

Friday's snow was no longer pristine. Over the weekend, thousands of tires had turned the streets and boulevards into mushy brown stew that enriched car washes. My windshield washers worked overtime. I parked on the street in front of the address and stepped into three inches of goop. Yuck.

Peter Born lived two miles from Art Kruger in a more upscale neighborhood. He and Art had served together in 'Nam, and they shared a bond that those who weren't involved couldn't understand.

"Even now I wake up sweating and shaking," he shouted. "Didn't used to happen."

"Usually you wake me," added his petite wife, Rose, nodding. "But, anyway, this is not what she's here for, Pete." She rose from her chair. "Would you like coffee or tea? I'll fix some while you two take care of business. And turn on your hearing aid, Pete," she advised on her way to the kitchen. "You don't have to bellow at her."

To the sound of coffee beans grinding in the kitchen, Peter and I worked through the interview form, he getting off track occasionally to reminisce about Art Kruger and how he would miss him. When I asked him about Jim Martin, however, his voice took a sharper edge.

"Jim Martin is a bigoted old goat. He's either getting senile or just plain going off his rocker. Aside from cards, I don't have much to do with him anymore. Don't know what happened to him."

Rose returned with almond-scented coffee served in delicate china cups with saucers. She resumed sitting in her floral wing chair and asked, "Did he tell you about the stuff they eat when they play cards? Potpies and store-bought cookies. Sometimes those high-fat salty deli meats and white bread. No wonder they're all sick. Such disgusting food. Though poor Jim got weaker and weaker this past year. Maybe he was eating too much junk food, and it killed him." She smiled and took a sip of her coffee.

"So, specifically, what did you all eat when the four of you were together last week?" I asked. "All I found in Mr. Kruger's refrigerator was some potato salad and sliced ham and deli foods in Mr. Martin's refrigerator. Was any of that food eaten when you played cards?"

"Of course not," Rose interrupted. "Even that disgusting stuff would be better for them than those ridiculous potpies. Who eats those things anymore?" Without taking a breath, she answered her own question. "Nobody taking care of their health would eat that stuff. It's no wonder you were sick. What did you tell her you ate? Did you tell her the truth?"

"Yes, my love. You do take good care of me. But once in a while," Peter assured her, "just once in a while, a piping-hot potpie is delicious. Especially when it's cold outside."

"I suppose it's fine as long as it's just once in a great while, Pete." Rose reached over and touched his hand, batting her eyelashes in a way I didn't think people in their seventies still did. I felt it was time to take control of this conversation before the two of them left for the bedroom.

"So the four of you had potpies and packaged cookies last week, is that correct?" I directed the question to Peter, avoiding Rose as much as she would let me. "What kind of potpie? What brand? Where did you buy it, and what brand of cookies did you eat?" I figured if I talked fast enough, Rose wouldn't be able to interject.

Ah, but I was so wrong.

"Well, I can assure you I would never, ever buy such unhealthy stuff." Rose continued with further analysis. "Did you ever look at the salt in a potpie? And the fat?" She grimaced and took another sip of her coffee. "The men are pretty sneaky about buying those nasty things." She barely inhaled before badgering her husband. "Where *do* you shop for them?"

"Ah, come on, Rosie. You know perfectly well that we only do this about twice a year. And I buy them at the same place you get our groceries. You just don't look hard enough."

"To continue," I interrupted, "what brand did you purchase, and what type of potpie was it?"

Peter was sure it was called Baker's Best and recalled it was chicken in gravy with peas and carrots. He added they heated the pies in the oven for about thirty minutes. I asked what temperature the oven had been, and he had no idea. We worked on the remainder of the questionnaire with minimal interruption from Rose. He thought that Art Kruger had brought the cookies but wasn't sure about that either. He also admitted there weren't any leftovers to sample. Rose had tossed it all after the other men left.

I hit the jackpot when Peter recalled, "You know, Art might have one of those potpies left in his freezer. He took the last two home with him."

How did I miss that? Did I look in Art Kruger's freezer? Would a frozen potpie have drawn suspicion anyway?

Who knows what lurks in potpies? There was a time when we thought food had to be contaminated with tens of thousands of bacteria to make people sick. Then it was discovered it only took five to ten microscopic *E. coli* bacteria in an undercooked hamburger to make an adult miserably ill or kill a child. Ten years ago, potpies were implicated in a salmonella outbreak. Why not potpies again?

# 12

I finished the interview with Peter and Rose Born and drove back to the Kruger house, hoping Marjorie was there and I'd be able to check the freezer.

No one answered the door, but I knew Marjorie had cleaned out the kitchen, and it was possible she may have already thrown out a lot of the food. While dumpster diving is not in my official job description, it seemed like it might fall under the task of gathering food samples.

I removed a pair of vinyl gloves and some plastic bags from my briefcase and walked around the house to the back alley. The garbage can was stuffed to the top, and its partially opened lid offered a scavenger's intriguing peek at the treasures inside. At least in the winter, food waste was too cold to rot and get buggy and pungent and totally disgusting.

Lacking a tarp or other large sheet, I just dug stuff out and put it on the plowed surface. Before I had barely begun the trashcan treasure hunt, Dorothy Martin came to her back gate. "What are you doing in Art's trash?"

"Dumpster diving," I replied with a smile. "Looking for frozen potpies."

She frowned. "What do you want with potpies?"

"Well, according to Peter Born, the guys in the card club ate potpies last week."

"Humph," she muttered. "Stay out of my trash, or I'll call the police."

It was less than five minutes later when the squad car appeared. The patrol cop exited his car and looked at my mess.

"What the heck are you doing?"

At this point, the sassy reply of "dumpster diving" seemed inappropriate. I gave him my name and produced my Health Department ID. "Looking for some potpies that might be related to a foodborne illness case and a death," I answered, businesslike.

He looked skeptical. "You're scrounging through a garbage can to find a potpie? Is this a joke?"

I assured him it wasn't a joke and produced my government-issued cooler and paperwork. He laughed. "And I thought my job had shitty duties." Then he retrieved a pair of disposable gloves from the squad and helped me sift through the garbage until I found an intact packaged potpie, still frozen solid. I stuck it in a bag, and we both tossed the rest back into the can.

"Best you're not out here after dark," he advised as he climbed back into his squad.

I took his advice, drove straight to the office, and delivered the sample to the waiting lab technician.

# 13

After dinner, I poured a glass of port and snuggled into my cozy chair. Dude curled himself into my lap and commenced his contented purr. "Well, guy, what do you think I should do?" He continued to vibrate, taking no interest in my problem.

I'd been thinking about how to apologize to Thomas for the abrupt dismissal I'd given him Saturday night. It was a rude response to his innocuous comment: "Trust me." David, my ex, had uttered those words what seemed like a thousand times from his drunken hazes, and I had wanted desperately to believe him. Finally, at one thousand and one, I found the nerve to walk away, thinking I could never trust anybody again.

The divorce had been bitter and drawn out because he didn't want to lose his enabler and punching bag. His parents refused to believe their son could be addicted to alcohol and be abusive. No, they all decided, *I* was really the problem in the marriage. David's parents had money and bought a good lawyer. I left with a suitcase, bruises, and a cracked rib.

"So, Dude, do I explain all this to Thomas, or just lie

and tell him I had a sudden migraine?" Dude lifted his head, squinted, and twitched his whiskers. "Trouble is he knows how to recognize a lie. What do you think?"

The cat lifted his butt off my lap and stretched, kneading his paws on my thigh.

It was pretty obvious he didn't care either way.

⟋

Art Kruger's obituary and funeral arrangements were listed in the Tuesday morning paper. The visitation was in the evening from five to seven. I uploaded the address and time on my phone calendar, thinking his daughter Marjorie might appreciate a familiar face.

Franklin and Jake were discussing the potpies when I walked into the office. I tossed my coat on my desk and joined them.

"This shouldn't be happening again." Franklin looked over Jake's shoulder at the screen. "The manufacturers were supposed to fix that problem after the last outbreak."

"Maybe, maybe not," Jake countered. "I've had one or two of those things in the past year and recall the dough was raw and the instructions just required heating in an oven at four hundred degrees. Never anything on interior temperature."

"It wasn't that long ago when frozen cooked chicken breasts caused an outbreak."

"Yeah, Laura, but they weren't fully cooked," Jake reminded me. "And maybe the chicken potpie wasn't either. Maybe there's gross contamination in the factory. Somebody isn't paying attention to quality control."

"We should hear something from the lab this afternoon. Until then, keep digging." Franklin stood to leave. "Laura, any more of those card players get back to you?"

"One of the remaining two. Jake has the interview form. Oscar Larson's wife hasn't been very helpful. Says her husband can't remember things. I'll give her another call today and ask about the potpies."

I returned to the pile of Javier's documents on my desk. I was rearranging them into delivery invoices and sales information by dates when the phone rang.

"You wanted to know if we took anything from the dumpster?"

It took a moment for me to recall my message to Thomas. "Yes, we're looking for more invoices, in particular from a place called . . . " I shuffled through one pile and pulled out the invoice, "called Ricardo's. We think it's a phony company that Javier made up to throw us off the traceback."

"Yes, you may be right." He sounded cold and distant, not that I could blame him after my Saturday night dismissal.

"Have you found anything to help us? That's all I really wanted to know."

"Might have," he offered. "Let's discuss it at lunch." We set up a place and an approximate time.

The billing statements weren't going to disappear, so I spent another hour sorting. Charges for products received, cash register readings of counter sales, and Javier's own invoices to the retailers he supplied. Some numbers didn't seem to jibe. The total sales receipts didn't look adequate enough to pay the invoices for two weeks. He'd ordered boxes and boxes of sausage casings. Even simple math could prove he hadn't sold that many sausages. I knew his business was good, but these numbers seemed out of proportion.

I red-inked a note on the list before sending it to Ag. They could use their whizzy formulas to figure it all out. There were no additional invoices from Ricardo's. I hoped Thomas would provide at least a hint to help me out.

# 14

The Downtown Deli sat on the banks of the Mississippi River, where the view was beautiful any time of year. The river was still flowing, not yet cast into a winter sleep by freezing temperatures and long, cold nights. I had just secured a table when Thomas arrived.

"You made it."

"Think I wouldn't?" He pulled out the opposite chair and sat down.

I felt a sharp pang in my gut. "I just know how busy it gets for you." I hurried on before my better sense would stop me. "And I really do need to apologize for last Saturday night. I'm sorry. I reacted badly, and some time I'd like to explain but not today."

"No, not today," he agreed.

A waitress put the menus on the table, and we ordered before she walked away. Lunch at the deli was not a time for relaxing conversation. Often there's a line out the door, encouraging guests to eat and get moving so everyone can get back to work.

"You wondered about the records we retrieved from the dumpster. I can confirm there were documents from a business named Ricardo's. We're looking into it. I can also tell you we've interviewed six employees, and there's one we can't find. Javier didn't keep accurate employment records. At least two said they were always paid in cash. And I can also tell you Javier's wife and son showed up this morning. That piece of information has been released to the media."

"Can we at least take a look at the paperwork?"

"Ask Franklin and the state health commissioner to contact the city attorney. That's all I can offer."

Our sandwiches arrived, and we ate hurriedly, exchanging mundane comments about the weather. Thomas gulped his last drops of coffee, put a ten-dollar bill on the table, and rose to leave. "I'll take you up on your offer for the explanation."

With that bit of relief, I paid the check and walked between puddles on the sidewalk to my car. The sun had come out, and the ice was melting. Now, instead of ice and snow, it was just a salty mess.

There were two inspections on my afternoon schedule, starting with Sir Pedro's on Lake Street. The restaurant had a history of problems and was under new management. Again. And they promised to improve. Again.

I knew something wasn't right as soon as I asked for the manager. It took over five minutes for him to emerge from the kitchen, and his voice was quivering with either surprise or fear. Maybe both. He introduced himself as Manny, the new manager.

"Now not a good time," he said, shaking his head. "Too busy."

I looked around the dining room. Lunch rush was over, and there were six people eating. Experience told me something was going on in the kitchen he didn't want me to see, and I'd better find out what it was in the next two minutes.

"Manny, the inspection will be done now. I won't interfere with the workers' tasks." I tossed my winter coat on a chair, pulled a clean white jacket from my briefcase, put it on, and opened my computer.

After a stop at the hand sink, I started the inspection on the steam table line in the kitchen, taking temperatures of cooked beans, shredded chicken, and cheese sauce. All were within the safety zone—a good start. I nodded at Manny, and he returned it with a tight smile.

Manny's English appeared marginal when he responded to my questions, but I suspected he understood a lot more than he was letting on. On the other hand, my Spanish was *muy poco*, very little, and while I had enough words to manage very basic communication, I most often didn't understand the answer.

We went into the walk-in cooler, where I found a five-gallon plastic bucket of refried beans at 55 °F. I asked when they had been cooked. "*Qué dia frijoles cocina?*" ("What day he cooks the beans?") The verb tense wasn't correct, but I was sure he knew what I was asking.

"*No sé, senorita.*" He opened the cooler door and called a cook. That's when I discovered he was lying.

I knew enough Spanish to recognize days of the week,

months, a few numbers, and some verbs. The cook answered the beans were cooked *sabado*, Saturday. But, in English, Manny told me Monday. Yesterday. Which meant the beans had been fermenting in the bucket for three days. I tried to explain why the beans weren't safe to eat. The cook understood my directions: *basura*. Garbage. He carried the bucket out of the cooler.

I spotted at least two dozen large unlabeled cardboard cartons of product on the bottom shelf. *"Qué está aqui?"* My suspicious nature was now fully engaged. "What is here?"

"Ah," he fumbled, "ah, *es chorizo*."

"That's a lot of chorizo." I moved a box to look for identification. Before I could pull it out, Manny yanked it out of my hands and shoved it back on the shelf.

"No. Not today."

If there's a true color for death warmed over, Manny was a poster boy. But he also looked determined to keep me away from the boxes. At that moment, the cook reentered the walk-in, and I had a sudden chill that wasn't from the refrigeration fans.

I knew if I demanded to see what was in the boxes, the two larger men would outmuscle me, and then what would happen? A safer choice was to return with reinforcements. In the past, I had dealt with one especially loud, in-your-face restaurant owner who threatened me, and I came with a patrol cop the next time. It seemed like a better option. The three of us exited the walk-in cooler.

I finished the inspection with no more discussion about chorizo. In addition to six other serious violations, the lack of cleanliness was disgusting. The floor looked like it hadn't been mopped for a week. A buildup of black gooey stuff under one prep table looked even older. Mice left a trail of evidence along a wall in the dry storage area.

Manny reverted back to Spanish for the remainder of the inspection. "*Sí, senorita, sí, sí.*" I gave him twenty-four hours to correct the critical violations and three days for the others. I advised him if there were any illness complaints in the next week, he would be closed for a hearing. I gave him Spanish-language food-code fact sheets for cooling and for hot and cold hold temperatures. He signed my form, took the information, and disappeared into his office.

As I packed the computer into my briefcase, I caught a whiff of a vaguely familiar men's cologne that often triggered an unwanted headache. I hurried out of the kitchen, passing an employee, who quickly turned his head to avoid my glance.

I did one more short inspection at a bakery and then drove back to the office to upload the reports. The boxes of chorizo still bothered me. What if they had come from Javier's market? If Javier had made sausage from unapproved meat, he wouldn't attach his name to the box, and he would make a nice profit avoiding legal meat inspections. The restaurant would purchase the sausage at below market price, increasing profit but risking customer health.

⁓

The sun settled into darkness, and the November night was not gentle. Car lights punctured the cold blackness with brutal efficiency, pushing the gloom aside. I wanted to go straight to my apartment but had promised myself to stop at the funeral home. Only six people signed the visitors' book before I arrived, and Marjorie was standing alone, staring at the casket. She didn't seem surprised to see me.

"Thank you for coming, Laura." Her thin smile started to droop at the corners as a tear ran down her cheek. "He did squeeze my hand ever so slightly."

I gave her a hug, understanding full well what was going through her mind, what she had lost. "I'm so sorry. This shouldn't have happened." What else was there to say? My emotions were ranging from sorrow at the loss of Marjorie's father to anger that a veteran who faced life-threatening hazards in Vietnam died from eating contaminated food in his own country.

As other mourners arrived, I slipped out into the dark parking lot and into my cold car for the drive home. A large pickup truck pulled out behind me and followed too close to my back bumper for my comfort. After four blocks, I pulled over to let him pass, only to discover the driver also slowed and then pulled into an empty space along the curb. Was he following me, or was he just a jerk?

# 15

Dude offered his unsolicited opinion on my later-than-normal arrival. His dish was empty, and he didn't stop nagging until I opened his can of Fancy Food, dumped it into his bowl, broke it apart with a fork, and set it in front of his particular nose. He could be starving, but if the food variety wasn't to his liking, he twitched his whiskers in disgust and kept howling for something else. Tonight the offering was satisfactory.

I flipped on the TV to catch the local news and saw a reporter talking about Javier's murder. She related his wife and son had arrived today from a trip and were devastated to learn of the death. "Police are talking with them right now," she continued from her post on the sidewalk in front of city hall. Then she dropped a bombshell.

"Our own Channel Twelve investigation discovered that this past April, Javier paid cash for his one-point-two-million-dollar house, and we believe the police are asking his widow about the transaction as we speak."

Javier couldn't have made that kind of money operating a small meat market in an ethnic neighborhood. I began to wonder if, as Thomas suspected, he was involved in drug distribution and if a rival eliminated the competition. All this certainly made our little project finding condemned pork carcasses more interesting. How did it all fit together?

The cell phone interrupted my musings. "Laura, I have some bad news," Franklin announced. "Jim Martin died this afternoon. The DNA from his and Art Kruger's salmonella are the same. We have to shift our priorities."

When he stopped for a breath, I grabbed the opening. "We need to get the potpie checked asap. It's the one food both those guys ate."

"I want you to reinterview the survivors of the card group. Get into the nitty-gritty, even down to added pepper."

"Okay. I'll see you in the morning."

"Seven o'clock. We have a lot to do." He disconnected.

Dude rubbed against my legs, expecting to be petted and reassured of his prowess and irresistibility. I wasn't in the mood. The phone rang again. It was Thomas.

"See the news tonight?"

"Yes, and am I guessing correctly that drugs might be involved?"

"That's a good guess." He went on. "I've got a question. Do you recall a newer employee in the meat market within the past two to three months?"

"Thomas, I wouldn't know. I wasn't there that often."

"We're still missing one guy who worked there. According to the others, shortly after he arrived, things started to change. He and Javier often stayed after closing hours, and the other employees thought the two were cutting meat and making sausage because the equipment wasn't always clean in the morning. It made some of them mad because they had to clean up the mess, but Javier just waved off their complaints. They thought the new guy had too much influence with Javier."

"Are you thinking he was part of the supply ring or one of Javier's distributors?"

"That's what we're looking into, Laura. Remember, if you find anything in those records that seems out of the ordinary, let me know."

"And you have records from the dumpster that we can't see."

"Mine's a criminal investigation. Yours is not."

# 16

Franklin made two columns on the white board in the meeting room. In the left column, he wrote two names: *Art Kruger and Jim Martin—confirmed salmonella. Deceased.* Under this, he wrote, *What do we know?*

At the top of the right column, he wrote, *Missing carcasses. Uninspected meats? What is our role?*

And that's how we began our morning, detail by detail. Jake started with the lab reports on the salmonella and results from telephone complaints.

"We've had four calls from sick people that might be related to this outbreak. Two of them are dropping off stool cultures at our lab today. I've loaded the salmonella DNA on PulseNet. It'll tell us if this is a national outbreak or just our very own Minnesota problem. If another state posts a matching DNA, then we're looking for an interstate food manufacturer, and it's time to call the federal inspectors.

"Our lab has alerted local clinics and hospitals to watch for salmonella," Jake continued. "The potpie tests are almost done. We should have some data by late this afternoon. We're calling local and outstate hospitals and clinics, but it takes time to get their data. The source is out there." He finished talking and crumpled his empty pop can.

"Laura, have you interviewed the fourth card player? Two are already dead, and I don't want to see another obituary."

"No, Franklin, I haven't. His wife was unwilling to cooperate over the phone. I'll just have to ring the doorbell and hope for the best."

"When?"

"Right after this meeting." I could tell from the frown that he was not pleased.

"Take Jake with you."

"Okay." I looked down at the paperwork, embarrassed at my lack of follow-through.

"And as long as we're picking on you," Franklin continued, "what's the latest on Javier's Market? Has Ag had any luck tracing the missing meat? Do they know where it came from?"

"I'm meeting with the team from Ag again tomorrow. They're still trying to trace the supplier of the carcasses. It's almost certain the company is either unlicensed or doesn't exist at all. Javier may have made those invoices himself before his hearing. Plus, there's a new angle." I directed my comments to Franklin, avoiding the anticipated glare from Jake. "Thomas thinks drugs are involved and Javier was a distributor. He'd like us to compile the information we have and look for abnormalities."

Franklin gave me a stern look. "He can have our data when we're done. We don't have time to do police work. We're investigating this outbreak. Period." He wrote *police matter* in the second column.

I got the message.

Jake outlined the food histories of the two dead men and Peter Born. He felt certain the men's card club was the source of the salmonella, possibly from improperly heated potpies. He also wondered if the men had remembered absolutely everything they'd eaten in the four days before they became ill. Franklin thought reinterviewing Peter Born and talking to the fourth member of the group was critical. Jake and I left the meeting to pursue card player number four, Mr. Oscar Larson.

Janet Larson answered the door with a distrustful squint that implied *what now?* "Yes?"

Jake smiled, introduced us, and explained why we had come and the very real urgency to interview her husband. Janet did an appraising sweep of Jake from head to foot and returned the smile. She barely glanced at me after that. We entered the cozy bungalow near Lake Nokomis on the south side of Minneapolis and shed our winter gear.

"We really feel awful about losing Art," she lamented while hanging our coats. "He was a good man. He and Oscar go back a long way. But as I told the woman on the phone, his memory isn't very good anymore." The fact I was the woman on the phone had totally escaped her memory.

Oscar Larson gave the impression of someone who knew how to take charge. He invited us into the living room and directed his wife to make coffee for their guests. "Please have a seat," he yelled and gestured to the subtle gray and blue upholstered sofa as he sat on the black leather recliner. Either his hearing aids were not turned on, or the batteries were dead.

"We both feel just terrible about losing Art. He and I go way back, you know. Talked to Marjorie at the funeral home. She's devastated, of course. But Art was having health problems, you know, so it's not a total surprise."

"Mr. Larson," I interrupted his musing, "we know Art Kruger and Jim Martin died from salmonella poisoning, and it most likely came from food you all ate at your card club gathering."

"Jim is dead too? When did that happen? My god. Hey, Janet," he shouted toward the kitchen, "did you know Jim Martin died too?" He directed his questions back to me. "When did this happen? We haven't heard anything about it."

"Poor Dorothy is probably just happy to be rid of him." Janet reentered the room.

"Janet," Oscar barked. "What a thing to say."

"It's true, and you know it." She glared at her husband before returning to the kitchen.

Oscar stared into a distant corner, lost in his thoughts. "Something happened to Jim as he got older. Got nastier, meaner. Sad to say . . . " He drifted off.

"Oscar," I pursued, "we don't want to intrude upon your time any more than necessary. Can you just help us with this food history interview so we can find out what may have killed both men?"

"Sure, honey. Whatever you need."

I removed the form from my briefcase and began interviewing him while Jake eased out to the kitchen to assist Janet with the coffee and to chat.

Oscar Larson didn't appear to have any memory issues as his wife had contended. "We had some popcorn and beer while we played cards. I brought the popcorn—you know, that bagged stuff already popped, buttered, and salted. I ate most of it, which was probably why I was too full for much potpie. Don't know why Pete likes potpies so much. At least twice in the winter, he brings them to our card club. It's his secret junk food, I guess. Rosie is darn picky about their food."

"Do you recall how they were heated?"

"Sure. We stuck them in the oven while we played a round or two. They were brown on the top and kinda bubbly, so we figured they were ready to eat. Mine was a little cold, so I nuked it to get it warmer."

"You stuck it in the microwave for how long, do you think?"

"Maybe two minutes. I know it was boiling hot, and I had to wait for it to cool before I could eat it. Pete ate about half of his and nuked the rest of it too."

"What about Jim and Art?"

"Nah, they just gulped them down like they hadn't eaten in a week. Art didn't have anyone to cook for him, and, well, you know, Jim's wife wasn't much of a cook either."

Janet and Jake brought four coffee cups into the room while Oscar discussed the food preferences of the two deceased men. Jake continued the interview.

"Would you be aware if either Art or Jim regularly ate frozen potpies?"

Oscar took a sip of the hot coffee and thought about the question. "Probably not. Art likes the frozen dinners. He had a lot of those black containers piled up in his kitchen. Jim ate a lot of deli foods. Like I said, Pete was the potpie guy."

Jake asked a few more questions to complete the interview and then asked if we might contact him again should we have additional questions.

"Sure, anytime. Just give me a call. I'd be happy to help."

Janet left to get our coats, and Oscar whispered to Jake, "Better if *you* call. The wife gets jealous when women call for me."

# 17

"Well, that explained a lot." I pulled the seatbelt over my shoulder and snapped it on. "People that age are still jealous?"

"Sure. Why not? My dad gets jealous whenever Mom gets a second look. They're still completely in love. Why shouldn't it endure? It's what marriage is all about."

I was envious of couples who had such great joy and longevity. My promise of happiness had been a nightmare as gloomy as the gray skies and the dirty snow on the boulevards.

Changing the subject, I asked, "Care to stop in at a problem place with me? Sir Pedro's needs their twenty-four-hour follow-up. They're hiding something. Maybe we can divide and conquer."

"Sure. What's the background?"

I explained yesterday's inspection, the long delay for the manager to appear from the kitchen, the suspicious boxes of chorizo he pulled from my hands, the lie about the day the beans were cooked. Today I planned to confirm the restaurant had corrected critical violations, those contributing directly to foodborne illness, and try to get another look inside the cooler, though I suspected the boxes would be gone.

We left our coats in the car and scampered to the delivery door, found it unlocked, and walked into the kitchen. We both showed our ID cards and asked to see the manager. An employee who appeared to be a cook scurried out to the dining room, his nose twitching like a mouse trapped in a maze. Another employee washing dishes slid behind a column, pulling his hat down over his eyes. Before we could wash our hands and start the inspection, the dining room door flew open at the hand of Miguel, who confirmed he was the restaurant manager today and demanded to know what the intrusion was all about.

"I told your manager Manny I would reinspect the critical violations today. He signed the report, and I emailed the entire document to the restaurant account late yesterday afternoon. Surely someone in charge must have read it by this time."

"Manny does not work here anymore, and I do not have that report. Maybe he threw it away."

When I produced my laptop to show him the signed report, Jake disappeared into the walk-in cooler, shadowed by the twitchy cook. Miguel scanned the document, and I joined the party in the chilly refrigerated box.

"Cooked bean temperatures OK?"

Jake was hovering over the shoulder of the cook, who was now looking at his thermometer in the bucket of beans. "Doesn't look too good, does it? You just told me these were cooked earlier this morning, correct?"

The cook shrugged his shoulders. "Maybe."

"Well, I'm confident you didn't cool these beans properly before you dumped them into the five-gallon bucket because the temperature is ninety-six degrees. Makes no difference if they've been in here over four hours or ten hours. It's long enough for bacteria to multiply fiftyfold. So we're just going to dump these into a garbage can right now." Jake used his cell phone to take a photo of the thermometer in the beans and then picked up the heavy pail and pushed the cooler door open. "Explain to him," Jake told Miguel as we walked out of the cooler.

I looked at the empty shelves where the chorizo had been stored yesterday.

Jake found a gallon of bleach and poured it over the pinto beans in the garbage can, making them irretrievable for consumption after we left. He handed the empty bucket to the cook. Then he surprised me with his halting Spanish as he advised the cook on cooling procedures. The cook appeared less than interested.

"Miguel," I asked, "what happened to the boxes of chorizo? Certainly you didn't serve all of it in twenty-four hours."

Miguel's face lit up like he'd swallowed siracha. "I don't have boxes of chorizo," he insisted. "You *loca.*"

"There were over a dozen cases of sausage in that cooler yesterday. Did you wholesale them to another restaurant?"

"No!" he shouted. "No chorizo."

Almost out of range, I could see another kitchen worker staring at us. Like the others, he wore a white jacket over jeans and a baseball cap with the restaurant's logo. He made no move to leave the kitchen with the other staff.

"Jesús," Miguel called to the onlooker. "We did not have cases of chorizo yesterday. *Sí?*"

Jesús pulled the cap lower on his forehead and took two steps closer. "No." He affirmed Miguel's denial. "Do you have pictures of these boxes that you claim were here?"

Jake and I exchanged wary glances. I opened my mouth to argue and discovered good reasoning instead. "I do not have photos of the boxes. Neither do I have photos of all the other violations on your inspection report. However, since yesterday's manager, Manny, signed the report, those issues are still on the table. And since you had the very same critical violation today, I will issue a citation and set a license hearing date for you within two weeks."

Jesús stepped a little closer. "We will correct everything, right, Miguel? It will not be a problem," he said with a thin smile.

Miguel's dark eyes darted from Jake to me to Jesús. "*Sí,* yes, we will correct everything."

The whiff of male cologne was unmistakable. Maybe it came from Miguel's fear-induced perspiration or from the more confident Jesús, but I recognized it immediately. "Okay, we're all settled. We both need to get back to the office." I nodded to the back door, and a puzzled Jake picked up the cue.

"Are you alright? What's going on?" Jake asked after we drove out of the parking lot.

I was breathing a little faster than normal, leaning against the headrest with my eyes closed. "Did you smell cologne? It's the same one I detected in Javier's office after his death. Whoever ransacked his office was wearing it."

"Laura, do you have any idea how many men must wear the same cologne? The probabilities don't hold water."

"Too much of a coincidence. Those boxes were there yesterday, that I certainly saw. This has something to do with Javier. I'm positive."

"Come on, Laura, you're reading way too much into this."

# 18

After the barista took my request for a medium dark chocolate mocha, I grabbed the Thursday morning paper and added it to the tab. While the milk steamed, I scanned the headlines, noticing one that read "Restaurant Robbery, One Dead." The inside story detailed a robbery the previous night at Sir Pedro's. Two armed men burst through the back door after the restaurant had closed and demanded the manager open the safe. According to the employees who were cleaning up the kitchen, the manager didn't move fast enough for the robbers, so they shot him, cleaned out one cash register, and left. The staff called 911, but it was too late for the manager, whose name was withheld until next of kin were notified.

I was certain Miguel was the victim. He had been too nervous, too unsure yesterday. He was a weak link.

My mocha came up. I whisked it off the counter and hurried to my car. Ten minutes later, I pulled into my parking space.

Jake was reading the paper at my desk when I arrived. "*Mea culpa*. You were right about Miguel. I don't think you should go back there by yourself. I've already talked to Franklin about it."

"You what? Don't you think I should have a say in this? I'm not a helpless female, you know. At the very least, don't you think I should have been present when you discussed this with Franklin?" I was mad enough to throw stuff. Good thing my mocha was gone, or Jake would have had a chocolate stain on the front of his shirt.

I turned around to find both Franklin and Thomas standing there. It was obvious we were having a discussion right now. Franklin pointed to the empty meeting room. When the door closed, Thomas took the lead, asking Jake and me about our encounter yesterday. After we described the limited inspection, he wanted more information about the missing boxes of chorizo and the reactions of the kitchen employees.

"Laura, did you recognize any of the employees from Javier's?"

"As I said before, no, I did not. I didn't inspect the market that frequently before the suspect carcasses came to light. I told you this, remember?"

"And you went back to Sir Pedro's yesterday, why?"

"Because they had serious critical violations with a twenty-four-hour correction time. It's standard procedure." I scowled at Franklin, anticipating his confirmation. "It feels like I'm on trial here." I crossed my arms and glared at them.

Thomas smiled, his dark eyes glowing in the morning sun that flooded the tiny space. "I like to verify the details twice, just to make sure the witnesses don't forget anything crucial."

"Witnesses," Jake and I exploded in unison. "What did we witness?"

"Little details that may help our investigation." Thomas put his notebook away. I swear he winked.

Franklin asked his own questions. "Do we send inspectors back there? If so, how soon? Is there anything else we can do to assist the police?" This from the man who decreed yesterday that we were not going to get involved in police work.

"The restaurant is closed while we investigate. I'm assuming you'll want to approve everything from a food-safety perspective before it can reopen." Thomas looked at me. "And if you do find anything suspect in the records from Javier's, we'd like to know that too. This information about the missing boxes of chorizo is helpful."

"Is it safe for her to go back there?" Jake asked.

Thomas hesitated a moment and noted my angry don't-even-think-about-it glare. "It'll be fine, but I'd prefer that two people do follow-up until *all* our investigations are completed." He looked at me for a positive reaction. He didn't get one.

As soon as Thomas was gone, Franklin asked about the documents from Javier's. "What progress have you made? Do you need help?"

"Any help you can spare. Ag guys have to be on this too. I'm still going through the dry product invoices."

Franklin called the commissioners of health and agriculture, and within fifteen minutes, we had assurances for all the help we needed to do a detailed analysis of Javier's records.

By noon, the box lunches were delivered, and six of us plunged into the piles of paper. Darren, Ag inspectors Scott and Henry, Jake and I, and a statistician from tech support got to work. The tech quickly had us organize information in a way that allowed her to enter the data into tables and make sense of it.

Darren produced estimates of whole carcass hog yields, including cuts of loin, bacon, spareribs, and sausage. If Javier had cut the carcass with those yields, we'd be able to justify that weight with the total pounds in his sales receipts. Jake and the Ag guys extracted numbers for the tech.

About an hour into our search, Darren rubbed his eyes and suggested a break. No one objected. He refilled his coffee cup. "How did you work this? All of a sudden we get this order from the top to get our butts over here and figure it out."

"Really? Butts?"

"Actually, it sounded more like 'get your sorry asses in gear or else.'" He smiled and took another swallow. "So precisely what is going on?"

I detailed my Tuesday inspection at Sir Pedro's and the now-missing boxes of sausage. Jake relayed our second inspection and Miguel's nervous reactions. I tossed the newspaper on the table. "Note the name of the restaurant."

"Drugs, I bet. I've heard rumors from some of the markets," Scott said. "A lot of the Latino operators have a good idea what's going on. They gossip. And they don't want to get sucked in."

"Do the cops think Javier was a major player who got hit by another dealer, or was he a minor cog like Miguel?" Darren asked.

"His house was worth over a million; does that answer your question?" Jake shook his head.

"Yep. It pretty much does." Darren pulled out several

delivery invoices from Ricardo's Meats. "By the way, Ricardo's Meats doesn't exist. Not that it's a big surprise."

Franklin opened the door and asked about our progress. "Keep at it. You're all on this until the work is done."

"While I'd like a break from inspecting, this is not quite what I had in mind," Scott replied to the now-closed door. He pulled another invoice from the pile. "Darren, what do you think of nonedible cellulose sausage casings? Would you use them for chorizo?"

"Maybe if you wanted skinless sausage. What's your thinking?"

"I'm thinking this guy Javier ordered a hell of a lot of cellulose sausage casings for a small meat market."

"I wondered about the same thing. And if you analyze his income versus his expenses, Javier didn't make any profit the last two months," I added.

By late afternoon, we'd found a definitive trend in Javier's records. He ordered a lot more casings than sausages sold. From his invoices, it also appeared he was supplying very large sausage orders to at least three local restaurants and several markets, including Sir Pedro's. None of us thought a restaurant could sell two hundred pounds of chorizo every day. As I wrote down pertinent info for Thomas, Jake answered a call from the lab.

"Thanks for the confirmation. We're on this." Jake put his phone on the table and filled us in. "The lab confirmed the salmonella from the potpie and from the dead men is a genetic match. Time for a heart to heart with the manufacturer."

# 19

Thomas was pleased to hear the summary of our afternoon's work. "This gives us another angle to investigate. Nice job." Before I could reply, he added, "I'll pick you up at your apartment in thirty minutes. We're going to a firing range. No refusals accepted."

"A firing range? I don't have a gun, Thomas. You know this. And I'm definitely not getting one. What's this about?"

"I just think it would be a good idea for you to be comfortable handling one. I worry about you when I know you're in unsafe areas of town."

"For your information, I grew up with a father who hunted, and I can handle a shotgun and a pistol, thank you."

"Okay, okay. I didn't mean to offend. But I need range time and just thought you might like to ride along. I'll throw in pizza."

"Dude needs to be fed first." I hesitated. *Do I really want to do this?* "And he needs a little love as well."

"How about I give him some TLC while you change?" The man would not be refused.

Three minutes after I had arrived in my apartment, one

minute after opening the can of cat food, the buzzer rang, and Thomas was on his way up the steps.

While I changed into jeans and a turtleneck, I heard Dude pouncing on the pile of tissue paper in the middle of the living room floor and Thomas yelling, "Gotcha," followed by more pouncing. My fair-weather feline was having too much fun with this detective.

The shooting range was located in the western suburb of Robbinsdale. Rush-hour traffic was heavy and slow. Thomas remained quiet while I filled the void with a lengthy description of the afternoon discoveries. He asked a few specific questions and then became silent again.

"You want the explanation, don't you? Why I asked you to leave so suddenly."

"I would appreciate it, yes."

I took a deep breath. "The words *trust me* are frightening. No. Actually, they terrify me. Every time he asked me to trust that he would change, I wanted to believe him, but I still ended up the object of his uncontrolled rage. You cannot possibly understand."

"Your ex."

"Yeah, my ex, David. Something I want to erase from my memory, but it creeps up now and then."

"Did you get some help afterward?" He focused on the road.

"Like a therapist, you mean?"

"Like that."

"Still am." I stared out the side window.

He was silent for a minute, watching the taillights of traffic in front of us and monitoring his mirrors. "You may not believe me, but I do understand. I've seen enough abuse in my job to realize the scars take a long time to heal."

I sniffed and pulled tissue from my purse.

"I can and will be sensitive. If you'll give me the opportunity."

"You want to date? Is that what this is all about?" Dabbing my eyes, I said, "I'm not ready yet, Thomas."

"Then can I have play dates with your cat?"

Our laughter pierced the emotional heaviness, and the tension dissolved. Thomas was the only man the Dude liked. Maybe I should take heed.

⁓

The indoor shooting range was crowded and noisy, and I was surprised at the number of women, easily over half. I wondered why they had purchased a gun and whether they expected to use it soon. Or did they have one just to feel more confident and secure? Then I wondered what I would have done with a gun in my doomed marriage.

Thomas found an open booth, hung our parkas, and removed his handgun from a pouch. He took a few shots at the target. "Wanna try?" He went directly into instruction mode, demonstrating how to handle, load, and hold the weapon. He stood behind me, reaching around to steady the weapon in my hands, his arms warming mine. Had he forgotten I knew how to handle one?

My bullet hit the outer edge of the center ring. He looked pleased.

"Very good. Try again."

"It is lighter and easier to handle than I expected," I admitted. "This can't be your service weapon. It's too small."

"It's my personal gun, a Smith and Wesson."

"Why do you need it? Isn't one enough?"

"I've had it a long time. It's my backup, Laura." He looked perplexed at my questions. "Try a few more shots."

Over the next ten attempts, my aim improved only by millimeters. "Enough. Your turn."

He removed his service weapon from the holster and shot off several rounds of well-placed bullets. I had no doubt he could shoot to kill when it was required.

"Feeling more confident?" He held my coat while I slipped my arms into the sleeves. "A few more times and you'll be very, very good."

"Barely passible." I laughed as we stepped into the cold night. "Thomas, you know this is all for naught, don't you? I will not be getting a gun. My job doesn't pose personal danger. One time, a lunatic bursts into a restaurant while I'm doing an inspection and points his weapon at everyone. Not just at me. At the cooks, the cashier, the customers. One time only."

"It could have been a bloodbath."

"But it wasn't a bloodbath. My chances of being injured in this kind of situation are nil. Nada. Not gonna happen."

"You may feel safe, Laura, and you will be nearly all of the time. I just worry about the one time it isn't safe. Walking into the back door of a kitchen unannounced in some neighborhoods is asking for trouble."

"In those neighborhoods, I go in the front door."

We climbed into the frigid car, and he handed the Smith and Wesson to me. "Put it in the glove compartment."

"Is the safety lock on?"

"Very good question—and time for another safety lesson." Again, he ignored my past experience and demonstrated as if I were a greenhorn. "I rotated the empty chamber to the top so it won't discharge if it falls or if someone hits it. You have to pull the trigger to rotate the cylinder, and then it will discharge." He handed it back to me. "Enough of this for now. Pizza as promised. Birch Pizza okay with you?"

"I haven't eaten there. Do we need a reservation?"

"Already have it."

"You were pretty sure about this nondate, weren't you?"

"I was hoping."

"Is it close enough to walk home?" I wondered aloud for his benefit. "Or should I plan on calling a cab?"

"Why?" he asked, followed quickly with, "Oh, yeah. How about I turn my phone off while we eat?"

"I can live with that."

# 20

We pulled off the still-crowded freeway and drove south on city streets. Plows had cleared the main routes and were now working the residential areas. Residents were required to move their cars to a previously designated side of the street before the plows came or look for their vehicle in the impound lot the next morning. Thomas took a detour to avoid the snow-removal equipment.

"You're a very cautious driver," I commented while he waited after the light turned green to look both ways before moving. "If I'd been behind you, I might possibly have laid on the horn. Not that I ever did that, of course."

"Streets are still a little slippery, especially the intersections. Never know if another car will slide right through. And if, as you say, you don't lay on the horn, I bet you don't run yellow lights either."

"Mostly never."

In the glow from passing headlights, I saw his smile. I relaxed, comfortable and safe. And hungry.

"What kind of pizza do you like?" he asked, reading my

mind. "They have a very good smoked pork and roasted red pepper. Does that sound appealing?"

"Sounds gourmet. Thin or thick—Thomas, watch out!" I screamed and instinctively flung my hands forward to brace myself on the dashboard.

A large orange city truck was coming straight at us over the center line. Thomas pulled the wheel to the right, trying to swerve out of its path, but the big steel plow smashed into the rear driver's side, pushing us over the curb and onto the sidewalk. The airbags exploded, slamming into my face with unexpected force. Sounds of more buckling metal and shattering glass pierced the air. A car alarm screamed.

"Laura," he yelled, "are you okay?" He had already opened his car door. "Can you find your phone? Call nine-one-one. Tell them an officer needs assistance and to send paramedics. I'll check on the truck."

Then I thought he said, "Get the gun out."

*What's he talking about? My face hurts. Are airbags supposed to work like this? Keep the gun handy? He's chasing the truck? Where's my purse?* My head was pounding. With shaky hands, I pushed the airbag aside, found the purse, and tried to open the zipper.

"I can't get it open," I shouted. No reply. "Thomas, where are you?" Still no reply. The zipper yielded.

I'd just finished relating our situation to the emergency operator when a dark pickup truck parked behind our wrecked vehicle. No one opened the driver's door for about thirty seconds, but when he did, he held a weapon in a manner that scared the hell out of me. He wasn't a cop, of that I was sure.

"Tell them to hurry up," I whispered to the 911 operator as I tried to shrink into the car seat. After pushing the airbag off my lap, I opened the glove box and removed the gun. I held it with both hands, finger on the trigger, not knowing what to expect or if I could even fire at another person. But as the dark figure came closer, anger roiled inside like I hadn't experienced for several years. I could and would fire the gun if my life depended upon it. I pulled the trigger to rotate the cylinder.

Two shots broke my concentration. In the mirror, I saw the stalking shadow turn toward the noise and raise his weapon.

Another gunshot exploded. Who had fired it? Then sirens screamed, and flashing red lights approached out of the darkness. At the same time, I heard Thomas yell, "Stop! Police. Drop your weapon." The shadow whipped around, fired three shots, and ran to his truck just as an unmarked police car slammed to a halt beside him.

A revolver came out the window. "I wanna see your hands."

When Thomas opened the car door, I still had an iron grip on the gun. "You're holding it right," he observed with a tiny smile as he pried it from my hands. "Are you okay?"

"Who is that? What was he doing? What just happened here?"

"I'm guessing he and the plow driver had the same agenda."

"But that's a city plow," I protested. "And who was shooting? You?"

"He resisted arrest, and he had a weapon. The plow ran

into two cars, and the driver ran down the street into an alley entrance. Patrol guys are looking for him. They said the plow was hijacked about an hour ago. Paramedics think the city operator has a broken rib and maybe a punctured lung."

"Did you kill him? The guy with the gun?"

"No, but he's been wounded. This was not an accident, Laura. It was intentional."

"Is this related to Javier?"

"It may be."

"That's certainly a definitive answer." I massaged my aching forehead.

"Are you okay?" he asked again, shining a light on my pupils.

"Quit." I brushed his hand aside. "Just get me out of here."

Thomas introduced me to the officer who would drive me home. "I'll call you when we're finished here. It'll be a while. Sorry about the pizza."

# 21

The exploding airbag left bruising on the right side of my face. I was moderately successful at covering it with extra makeup but still hadn't come up with a plausible explanation for the discoloration when I walked into the office the next morning.

Darren and five inspectors from Ag were digging through files, reviewing our list of meat markets and restaurants that purchased wholesale from Javier. Franklin committed four of our staff to assist, including Jake and me. The idea, as Darren explained it, was short, focused inspections in these locations, looking at hanging carcasses for USDA stamps and for wholesomeness, watching for cases of product labeled *chorizo* or boxes without labels. He also wanted us to look at packaged meats for the USDA label. If anything was questionable, Darren wanted it all confiscated.

"Darren, are you crazy?" I knew his approach would lead to more danger than he realized. "If a drug gang is involved, this isn't safe. Absolutely not safe. They aren't going to let anybody walk out with cases of drug-stuffed sausage casings. They have guns. We do not."

"Are we sure drugs are involved, Laura? That was a hypothesis, not necessarily factual. I'm after the uninspected meat to keep it out of commerce."

Darren sounded like a clueless government wonk, and I was almost ready to wipe off my makeup and show him the results from last night's accident. "Why don't we just condemn anything without an inspection stamp and take photos? If we see suspicious boxes, document them but don't make it obvious. If the manager seems nervous or defensive, get out of there. We can get a cop to go back in with us."

"I agree with Laura," Franklin announced from the back of the room. We all turned to look at him.

"But—" Darren started to object.

"But nothing. The safety of state employees comes first and foremost. Laura is correct. There's a very strong possibility that drugs were involved at Javier's. In fact, at this point, I'm not even sure you should do this surprise sweep."

He knew. Thomas must have called Franklin last night. If not then, certainly this morning. Franklin knew about the accident, and he was aware of the risks involved in Darren's plan.

Darren was not happy, having no choice but to agree with the new mandate. "Take photos and document," he now instructed.

"If anything feels even a little bit iffy, call me," Franklin added, assuming new leadership. "And get out immediately." The early rah-rah enthusiasm and laughter seeped out of the room like air escaping a dying balloon.

"Does one of you speak Spanish?" Franklin asked.

"*Sí. Hablo Español.* Not great but adequate." Kyle Peterson stood up. "Darren called me up from the poultry processing plants in Marshall. Been working with immigrants for five years. I can communicate."

"Okay. You bridge the language gap." Franklin continued, "On another topic, the potpies we believe caused the two deaths came from a local facility called Baker's Best. Laura and Jake, you two are going to join the federal inspectors in the factory where the potpies are made. We've had two complaints on the hotline that appear to be related, and there's urgency to find the salmonella source."

"Can't the feds just take care of it?" I asked.

"Yeah, that's their job," Jake protested. "We're needed on the meat market sweep."

"I'll decide who is and is not needed. Both of you get your paperwork together and meet the officers at the factory at nine o'clock. No more questions." Franklin stood to leave. "From anyone."

Not one of us was going to challenge the massive authority figure filling the doorway.

⁓

"What did you walk into?" Jake asked after we slid into the frigid state car that had been parked in the ramp overnight.

"Airbag," I replied without looking at him. As much as I'd hoped the heavy makeup would cover the discoloration, it apparently did not.

"What happened? Was anybody hurt? Beside you, I mean. How bad is the car?" He rambled on. "And why did you come to work today? You should have stayed home."

I answered his questions concisely, hoping to avoid the inevitable *who* question. "The car was hit by a snowplow. No one had serious injuries." I hedged on that answer because the city plow driver was still in the hospital from his beating by the hijackers. The guy who ran the plow into us had been shot and captured and was hospitalized under police watch. "The car is being evaluated today."

"Did you get a loaner, or will you need a ride to work? I mean I could just pick you up in the morning and drop you off after work. It's not too far out of my way."

"Oh, Jake, it is so out of your way. I'm south of downtown, and you're northwest burbs. Thank you, but I'll be fine." I changed the subject. "Does Baker's Best management know we are coming, or is this going to be a rude surprise?"

"The feds contacted them last night. I'd bet the factory staff is scrambling right now. They can't withhold records, but they might try to make them unavailable for a while. We'll see what happens. Franklin sent three interns out to purchase Baker's Best potpies from different grocery stores this morning. They'll be looking for the same code as the one on the box you pulled out of the trash, and they'll purchase newer dates so we can determine if the issue is ongoing or an error during one production period."

The freeway to the southwest suburb was the usual rush-hour stop, go, creep-along speed. *Rush hour* is really a misnomer. It's *hours*, with an S, and it can be two to three each way if the weather is bad or if you leave at exactly the wrong time. We left at exactly the wrong time.

Jake shook his head with regret. "We should have picked up coffee for this trek. But then we'd be even later."

# 22

Darren was not at all pleased that Franklin had usurped his lead on the meat market sweep. He was positive this was a case of uninspected carcasses moving through commerce, and this was his only concern. If Franklin and Laura's cop friend wanted to worry about drugs in chorizo boxes, then that was their problem. He was going to do his job and do it right. If boxes needed to be torn open to confirm the contents, they would be torn open. It was his raid. Besides, he was sure nobody would dare assault a State of Minnesota employee.

Early the next morning, two State Ag cars raced into an icy parking lot and slid to a stop next to the dumpsters behind La Carniceria. Darren and five inspectors piled out and rushed to the receiving dock of the market. Darren rang the bell and then pounded on the heavy steel door.

"Look, guys, I'm in charge here. We red-tag anything without an inspection stamp, and if you find sealed boxes that are questionable, open them. Got it?"

As the receiving door opened, Kyle sidled next to him. "Take it easy, Darren. We don't have all the facts."

"My case," Darren snarled.

A short, dark-haired man in dirty jeans and a plaid shirt peered past the security chain through a three-inch gap in the opened door. His eyes grew large and fearful when Darren presented his badge. Only after Kyle explained they were meat inspectors did the employee allow them to enter.

The inspectors marched through the dock storage area, heading for the meat-cutting room and sales cases. Their mass presence startled a lone shopper, who stood wide-eyed, observing the commotion. They opened their briefcases, pulled out white jackets and clipboards, and spread out like ants at a picnic, three to the meat cases, three to the walk-in coolers and packaging room. The startled employee frantically punched numbers on his cell phone.

"What's going on here?" a booming voice shouted from the grocery aisle. "Exactly who are you, and what are you doing? I'm calling the cops."

"We're State Agriculture inspectors," Darren announced, holding his badge. "We're looking for uninspected meat. Who are you?"

"Hernan Perez. I own this place, and all our meat has been inspected. We follow the rules. What do ya think? That we're stupid?"

Sensing an imminent confrontation, Kyle stepped in front of Darren and spoke to Hernan in his fractured Spanish. "*No se apuró. Él es un cabeza caliente. No estaremos mucho tiempo aquí. Okay, amigo?*" ("Don't worry. He is a hot head. We will not be here very long.")

"*Sí.*" Hernan raised his arms as if to say *whatever*, turned, and left.

"What was that all about?"

"I simply explained what we were going to do and why. It's easier sometimes to take a less confrontational approach." Kyle smiled at his lie.

"That's your opinion," Darren snapped, pushing him aside.

# 23

Jake pulled into the parking lot fifteen minutes late but still earlier than the federal inspectors, who also underestimated the commute time to the southwest suburbs.

Baker's Best Products was housed in an old concrete block building from the 1960s. Except for the glass entry doors, there were no windows on the first floor and a limited number on the upper story. It sat like an enormous gray casket on the edge of a small industrial area close to the freeway for easy transportation access.

"Think the inside looks any better than the exterior?" I shook my head.

In the small, dim reception room, a sole security guard asked us the purpose of our visit before calling for clearance. "Yeah, two from the State Health Department, Jake Schaffner and Laura Nielson," he advised, looking at our badges and driver's licenses. "They said they're expected, plus some other inspectors are coming soon." He listened to the reply. "You're not coming to escort? That's not protocol." He listened again. "Okay, if that's what you want.

"Meeting room two eighteen," the guard directed. "Second floor, turn right out of the elevator."

The meeting room was well lighted by eight-foot windows overlooking the parking lot and the adjacent white landscape hiding whatever remnants of fall colors lay dormant beneath it. In the middle sat a long, polished, dark oak table and gray cushioned side chairs exuding a calm that would soon be shaken by our presence.

We took a seat and waited.

Three minutes later, a thin young woman with stringy blond hair pushed the door open and mumbled, "Mr. Lundeen, the factory manager, will be late. I think some emergency or something has come up on the floor. Can I bring you coffee or something?" She was obviously nervous, rubbing and scrubbing her hands without the soap and water necessary to get rid of the falsehood.

"How long do you think it will be?" Jake asked.

"I . . . er . . . um, am not sure. Maybe fifteen minutes? Something like that."

"Really?" I replied with as much sarcasm as I could muster. "He did know we'd be here this morning. There are others coming soon. Perhaps you could remind him that this 'something' is important."

"Yeah, oh, sure, I can do that," she answered and rushed out.

Jake scowled. "It's not her fault. That was harsh."

"Some days I just get tired of excuses."

We waited.

"Sorry, sorry for the delay," Michael Lundeen apologized

as he pushed the door open twelve minutes later. His head and shoulders stooped over a stack of papers that he laid on the far end of the table. As he sat down, his brown cardigan sweater revealed the extra roll of fat burgeoning around his belt. Then all we could see was his partial balding and light-brown hair.

"I understand we may have a problem?" he asked, still inspecting his documents on the table.

Jake described the illness outbreak and how it was traced to the potpies, emphasizing that two people had already died from this particular species of salmonella. He pushed a copy of the Health Department lab reports across the table. "From your products. Look at the test results."

Michael scanned the report, threw it on the table, and shook his head. "This doesn't mean anything. How do we know it wasn't contaminated by the end user?"

"Because it was still frozen and intact in the carton when I collected it," I replied, addressing the bald spot.

"I suppose you want to see our records. We do use a lab, you know. And I think you'll find all our results are excellent. Your lab tests are either in error or bogus. Plus you don't really have any jurisdiction here. We're not licensed by the state."

His smugness melted like ice on a salted sidewalk when four USDA officials entered the office with their briefcases and official demeanor. A tired-looking, gray-haired man introduced himself as George and handed each of us his business card. After introductions, he told us we would spend two to three days in detailed inspections. Each would have an assignment, and we would be expected to keep precise notes. His staff would take apart machinery piece by piece, look for visible contamination, swab the food contact surfaces, and reassemble it. They would also be swabbing floor drains and sampling the water while Jake and I reviewed factory food safety operational standards.

Michael leaned back in his chair, allowing me a brief snapshot of his pasty white face before he raised a hand to hide his mouth.

Maybe he was going to vomit.

# 24

Darren and his raiders pulled up to their third establishment of the morning, a medium-sized grocery-butcher shop two blocks east of Nicollet Avenue. He directed three to use the front door, while he, Kyle, and another would enter from the back. As they exited their cars, a small white delivery van pulled away from the dock door and sped past, splattering them with brown slush and salt goop.

"Crap." Darren brushed the dirty, wet crud off his jacket. "Where is he going in such a hurry?"

Like soldiers on a mission, they marched to the back door, daring anyone to defy their authority. But the door was open, and there wasn't an enemy to conquer. One lone employee approached them. "Can I help you?"

While Kyle talked to the man, Darren and his crew were dismayed to find the meat cooler empty. The only fresh meats in the store were a few packages in the customer display case, a paltry amount for a business of this size.

"Kyle, ask him why they don't have any inventory. This isn't enough for ten customers." Darren was frustrated.

"He says the meat is gone."

"Where the hell is it?"

"*No sé.*" Kyle replied. "That translates into 'I don't know.' That's the only thing he says now. But I'm wondering about the white truck that sped out of here."

"Well, damn it," Darren fumed and slammed his clipboard on a stainless table. "He knew we were coming."

"Yeah, I'd say you're right," Kyle replied.

"They're not getting away with this," Darren continued to rage. "We'll divide and conquer. From this point forward, we use three smaller teams instead of one large one. Two of you stay here and find all their delivery receipts. Two others take this half of the market list. Kyle and I will take the rest. And warn everybody to keep an eye out for that white truck."

"How we gonna get back to the office?" asked a minion.

"Kyle or I will pick you up when you're finished and drop you at another market. We're going to find these bastards." Satisfied he had everything under control, Darren motioned to Kyle. "Let's get going."

# 25

While George and his staff donned white lab coats and began their investigation in the factory production area, I started with the small file of daily logs that Michael Lundeen had left on the table. The data only went back two weeks, and even then, there were too many blank spaces. I went in search of Michael and additional paperwork.

Jake was standing in the hall, talking on the phone, when I opened the door. He turned on the speaker so we both could hear.

"This morning, a Dakota County sheriff found eight carcasses dumped in a field about ten miles from Farmington," Franklin related. "The farmer drove out to check his stock and saw unfamiliar tire tracks in the snow. He followed them to a drainage ditch, where he found them. Apparently, coyotes had been gnawing on the frozen meat, but the farmer was still sure it was pig carcasses. He wants it all removed immediately. The Department of Agriculture will retrieve it. Ag wants samples to send to their Iowa lab for extensive testing, including DNA. They might be able to determine the breed and maybe the location the pigs were raised."

He continued the narrative. "The sheriff also said that a neighbor met a small white delivery-sized van driving slowly down the road three nights ago and was suspicious because only locals use that road at night."

"So we should be on the lookout for white delivery trucks?" Jake asked.

"No, you should not. We'll let the police handle it. Is that totally clear?"

"Uh-huh, sure. Got work to do. Thanks, Franklin." Jake disconnected.

"You don't seriously think you're going to search the streets of Minneapolis and St. Paul looking for white trucks, do you?" I asked.

"Nah, not exactly, but we'll keep our eyes open, partner."

"*Our* eyes? Hey, leave me out of this. I'm not going to be part of your crazy idea."

"Yeah, okay." He sounded disappointed. "Found anything in those documents yet?" He pointed to the folder in my hand.

"I don't like these sanitation logs. Too many empty spaces. They use pencil, and I also see too much erasing. If a corrective action is necessary, they should do it and document it. In ink. What about the lab reports? Do they do surface swabbing? Utensils, sinks, drains, things like that, or do they only test the potpies?"

"I've only reviewed lab reports for the chicken and gravy mix and haven't seen anything for the final product. Let me check another tab." Paging through the large black book of reports, he stopped to assess the information. "Here are some, but this is dated eighteen months ago. They must have more recent results in a different book."

My phone rang. I wasn't sure who was calling but answered anyway.

"Laura, this is Marjorie; you remember me? Art Kruger's daughter."

"Yes, of course I do. How are you doing?"

"I'm getting ready to leave. The house is listed, and I've hired an auctioneer to sell what he can. The rest will go to the Salvation Army. There's nothing more I can do here. Besides, it's too cold for my blood. I appreciate all your help. Thank you for everything."

"You do have legal avenues," I advised. "There are lawyers who specialize in foodborne illness litigation."

"I'll think about it. But it won't bring him back, and, frankly, I don't want to relive this. Dorothy, on the other hand, could use that kind of assistance. She had Jim cremated, you know. There won't be a funeral, just a visitation tonight. "

"Where is it?"I wrote the time and address in my calendar. "I'll try to stop in."

"Don't expect her to be grateful."

I thanked her for the warning and wished her a good trip.

"Jake, do you mind stopping at the visitation for Jim Martin on our way back? It's at the Jackson Funeral Home on Twenty-sixth Street."

"No problem. That's one of the card players who died, right?"

"Yes. His wife could use some support."

I grabbed my stack of papers and went in search of a quiet workspace away from Jake's mumbling and occasional expletive outbursts. I found a quiet but depressing space in the employee break room at the end of the hall—industrial gray floor tiles; grubby, long folding tables; old brown folding chairs, some with torn seat covers; and a coffee pot with three years of built-up scum. I put the documents on the table and went searching for Michael Lundeen and the missing records.

~

As much as he wanted to soldier on, Darren knew he'd have a revolt if they didn't stop for lunch. They parked in front of a small restaurant on Nicollet Avenue, an energetic area south of downtown Minneapolis called Eat Street, occupied by dozens of family-owned food establishments—Greek, German, Chinese, Vietnamese, Mexican, African, and Middle Eastern restaurants and groceries—available to satisfy every palate. It was a foodie paradise.

"Where are the other guys?" Darren asked as three of his army were seated at a booth in Amy's Chinese Restaurant.

"They broke rank. They want gyros."

After the lunch order for chicken fried rice and egg rolls was taken, Darren presided over a review of their findings. Aside from the market with little meat, they all appeared legitimate. He announced that tomorrow they would review all the records they had copied from the first market to look for irregularities, in particular delivery invoices from either Javier's or the phony wholesale supplier called Ricardo's.

"I doubt we'll find anything more today," Kyle advised. "After our first stops, the warnings went out. And some of them think we're ICE agents," he added, referring to US Immigration and Customs. "They've gone into hiding."

"I disagree. I think they just moved the illegal products to another market. No one knows we're trying to hit them all in one day."

*Star Wars* music rang from his parka pocket. "Yeah."

Darren listened as Franklin updated him. "We saw that vehicle this morning about two blocks from here. We'll keep a lookout for it. Thanks for the tip." He disconnected before Franklin could issue an order prohibiting van chasing.

"Eat up," he directed. "We've got some more places to visit. And you remember that white delivery truck that went racing out of the parking lot this morning? Someone used it to dump the old carcasses in a Dakota County farmer's field."

# 26

Jake shouted into his phone. "Presumptive salmonella? Why aren't you using the rapid tests?" Six seconds later, he exploded. "I understand the term *presumptive*. Was it or was it not positive for salmonella?"

Peeking into the meeting room, I gave him a quizzical what's-going-on-here look as he waved one arm in disgust and continued to shout.

"All I want is the precise date of that report. Surely you keep copies of all your lab work. Aren't you accredited? That's standard procedure." He listened. "Yeah, well, you get back to me as soon as you find it."

As soon as he hung up, he started ranting to me. "What a joke. I cannot believe some of this stuff. Missing dates, missing lab results. Some of these reports don't even have a signature. Look at this mess." He groaned, gesturing at the scattered piles in the middle of the table.

"Why don't I help you get them organized? I'll start with a pile for each year, and then we can break each year into months and dates."

We worked for an hour in silence, stacking and reorganizing the papers. Normally a factory this size would take food and environmental samples daily, but it was obvious that for some weeks either no samples were taken, or the records were missing. Jake was betting those records had not so mysteriously vanished to get rid of positive results.

While he continued to fume, I made a quick escape to the vending machine for two diet colas.

"Take a break and cool down," I advised, handing him a can. "Attorneys will be involved with this very soon, and subpoenas will be flying." I took a sip. "I'm seeing irregularities on the sanitation records that don't make sense either. And Michael is nowhere to be found. The office staff doesn't know where he is, so I'm stuck with only the documents he provided. Some of the entries are questionable."

Jake slammed his beverage can on the table. Pop exploded, splattering our neat stacks of records. "Two people died, and no one seems to care. I hate this."

I left him cleaning up the sticky mess and escaped to the break room to continue reviewing files. I was looking for an "aha" moment, a discovery that would send Michael Lundeen and everyone who'd collaborated with him to jail. The more I searched, the angrier I became.

Like the poorly documented lab results Jake had found, many of the daily sanitation reports were also missing, and several were not signed. Then there was the employee illness log, a requirement for every single manufacturing and retail operation that handles food. According to the log, not one of the seventy-seven employees working in the factory missed a day of work from illness in the past year. This was improbable.

My stomach was roiling by the end of the afternoon when the team of inspectors met to determine the next steps. George, whose last name I could no longer remember, asked if we had any questions.

"When was the last inspection here?" Jake asked before anyone else could get started. "You know, somebody should have seen these irregularities a long time ago. Your guys are responsible for this place. What have you been doing?"

"Not enough employees. No local lab support here either. We gotta send the samples from today to St. Louis. It's just the way it is," George answered. "I know. It sucks."

"And in the meantime, people get sick and die? Is that the way it is too?" Jake bent the empty cola can in half with one hand.

I sensed his irritation rising toward eruption. "What's the next step, George?" I hoped to slow Jake's lava flow but was in full agreement with his outrage.

"We'll seal this room for the weekend and come back Monday morning. We can't take their records with us, but we sure can lock them up." George pulled a ring with three keys from his pocket and held it up for our inspection. "All the keys to this room, courtesy of the maintenance supervisor. We'll post the door with a 'no entry' sign and lock it. Two of our guys will be here tomorrow to observe production and take more samples. See you Monday morning, early. Have a nice weekend," he added.

We zipped our down-filled jackets, pulled on gloves, and

walked into the dark chill. Jake's phone rang as we left the building. He fumbled to pull it out of his pocket and remove a glove so he could swipe the screen. "Yeah," he answered, still in a furious temperament.

Darren was shouting on the other end. "Someone slashed a tire, and we need a ride back to the office."

"Take a cab, Darren. We're out in the west burbs, and we have a funeral-home stop to make. Besides, didn't you ever learn how to change a tire?" Jake disconnected and unlocked the car. "What an idiot."

# 27

The only floral tribute for Jim Martin was a simple vase of flowers from the remaining two card players and wives. Nothing from family members or other friends. Not even a single rose on the urn. Dorothy wore a cobalt-blue dress and had obviously had her hair done in a salon. She looked a heck of lot better than the last time I'd seen her. She didn't assume the role of the grieving widow. In fact, she carried a discernible air of relief.

Jake and I recognized the four people talking to Dorothy. They waved at us like old friends.

"Find anything in those pies?" Peter Born shouted, apparently forgetting to turn on his hearing aids again. "Did they kill old Jim here and Art too?"

"Yes, the potpies were responsible for their illnesses," Jake answered in hushed tones, attempting to lower the decibels to funeral-home appropriateness.

"See? I told you those things would kill you." Rose Born elbowed her husband. "What saved these two?"

"Heating them thoroughly," I assured them. "Hot enough to kill the salmonella."

"Well, I'll remember that next time. Maybe I'll give you a call first," Peter bellowed.

"You're not eating those things ever again," Rose warned, raising her voice. "They are disgusting."

Dorothy now stood alone next to the unadorned ceramic urn on a small oak table. I approached and offered my condolences. "I'm sorry for your loss, Dorothy."

"Don't be," she answered without hesitation. "He was a beast, and everyone knew it. Even his own son won't come."

"Not even for you?"

"Do you see him anywhere?"

"Have you found resources to help you work through all the legalities and perhaps a social network to help with adjustment, something like a victim's advocate group?"

Pointing to the shadow of bruises on my face, she countered, "It doesn't look like you follow your own advice."

Jake and the two couples had moved their discussion to the back of the room. As I returned, he was describing details of tracking foodborne illness to his rapt audience. Rose Born kept jabbing an elbow into her husband's arm. "See, see? I told you so."

Catching my nod, Jake bid his new fans goodnight and followed me out. "How's Dorothy doing?" he asked, holding the passenger door open.

"Well, she's certainly happy to be rid of him, but once this is over, it doesn't appear she has any support system."

"She has those friends. They'll be there for her."

"Maybe."

While the car warmed up, we both checked our phones

for recent messages. Nothing on mine. In particular, nothing from Detective Garcia. *Isn't he at all interested in how I've been doing since the accident last night?*

"So someone slashed one of Darren's tires." Jake turned onto Lake Street. "Did he insult somebody else today?"

"It wouldn't be anything new," I answered. "But I'm guessing he was too close to the drugs. The tire was a warning. He needs to stop now before someone gets hurt . . . or worse. I wonder where it happened. Close to Javier's or Sir Pedro?"

"Didn't ask," Jake replied. "Wanna stop for a burger and a beer? Or I can loop over a few blocks for deli stuff. Which do you prefer?"

"How about something to take out? My cat is going to be yowling loud enough to bother the neighbors if I don't feed him soon."

"Come on. He'll survive. What's another half hour?"

"In cat time, it's too long."

"How about a quick soup and sandwich?" he persisted.

"As long as it's quick," I replied, caving to a stomach growl.

We stopped at a small family-owned restaurant and waited in the crowded entry area for a table to open. After twenty minutes of standing in the crush, we agreed to get takeout and had our sandwiches in less than ten minutes.

"Can I drop you at your place?" Jake made a right turn out of the parking lot.

"No, my car's in the office ramp. It wasn't my car in the accident. I was riding with someone else."

"That's lucky."

I detected skepticism in his reply.

Ahead, a small, unmarked white truck entered the street from the alley, tires spinning on an icy patch before the vehicle gained traction. "Think that's our guy?" Jake sped up.

"No, I don't think so, and we shouldn't follow it. Look what happened to Darren this afternoon."

"Let's see where it goes."

"Jake, I really don't think we should do this. If it has anything to do with drugs or pig carcasses, it could be dangerous. Besides, what makes you think this particular truck is delivering anything?"

"Just for a few blocks." He ignored my question.

At the next intersection, the truck turned left. Jake waited for oncoming traffic before bolting through the turn as the light turned red. The truck was now more than a block ahead of us, and I hoped it would disappear along with this reckless idea of pursuit. Then we saw brake lights as it turned right into a parking lot between two buildings.

Jake found a spot to pull over, where we watched the driver enter the side door of a restaurant. Within two minutes, he came back out, opened the back, unloaded several boxes onto a dolly, and rolled them into the glow behind the door. Minutes later, he returned, lifted the dolly into the truck box, pulled the door closed, and climbed in the driver's seat.

"What do you think they're delivering at this time of night?"

"Why don't we just let Ag and the police find out, Jake? We'll give them this address and the license plate number. It would be smarter."

"Yeah, we can do that, but let's follow for one more stop.

Don't you want to find out where he goes and what he has in the truck?"

"We're assigned to Baker's Best, remember?"

"Just one more stop." Jake turned on his headlights and pulled in behind the white truck. "Get that license plate, will you?"

I entered the information and the restaurant address on my phone. "I don't think you should get this close. He'll figure out you're following."

"Well, if he has nothing to hide, what difference does it make?"

"And if he has something to hide, then what?"

"You worry too much. The detective has you all upset about nothing."

"Thomas thinks there may be drugs involved, remember?" I shouted louder than necessary for the interior of a car.

"Are you seeing him?"

"No, I am not *seeing* him, if you're speaking in terms of dating. And even if I was, what difference would that make?"

"I'd worry about your safety, that's all."

"Just watch your driving," I ordered.

The white truck sped down the street, turned right at the next corner on a red light, and disappeared. Jake turned at the same corner and drove slowly, peering into parking lots, looking for alley entrances. Three blocks later, he spotted the truck backed up to the delivery door of a small grocery/meat market. The business was closed to customers, but a bright beam speared the darkness each time the door opened and closed. Jake parked across the street and kept the motor running to keep the interior warm. We hadn't exchanged a word in ten minutes.

"Get that address too," he finally directed. "We'll give it to Darren. And to the cops."

"I know this place. El Vaquero. It's in my inspection district."

At this stop, the driver picked up boxes and large bulky bags—my first thought was animal carcasses—and loaded them into the back of the vehicle. I wondered if the owner had either heard about Darren's raids and was getting rid of uninspected meat or if this had something to do with drugs. Maybe both.

"I don't think we should follow any longer, Jake. This could be risky. Plus, I would like to eat what's in this pretty soon." I held the white carryout bag to remind him of our purchases.

"Just one more stop," he promised, turning on the headlights. This time, the truck crept down the street, turned right, and then right again before pulling into a parking space along the curb. As we approached, the driver opened his door and jumped out.

"What's he doing?" Jake asked, as if I should know.

The driver wore a bulky gray parka with the hood pulled down to his eyebrows and the high collar zipped up to his bottom lip, masking his facial features. Aiming a large flashlight into Jake's eyes, he yelled, "Hey, you following me? Get outta here."

He stepped away and lifted his other arm to reveal a baseball bat. The left headlight exploded. Jake slammed our car into reverse, sped backward, and slid into a U-turn.

"Watch out for other cars," I gasped.

"We're good," he assured me, barely slowing at a four-way stop. Five blocks farther, it was obvious the van wouldn't follow.

"Drive to the Powderhorn Precinct office right now. We need to report this. I have the license plate number."

"Yeah, okay," Jake agreed and then moaned. "Franklin's gonna kill me."

# 28

By the time I returned to my apartment, I was mad at Jake, mad at the police officer who took more than an hour writing up our report, mad at Thomas for not calling, and mad because my takeout sandwich was squished. I poured a glass of wine and sulked.

Dude was my savior of the evening, curling into my lap and vibrating contentedly after getting an extra portion of roast chicken feast, which he deserved because it was so long after his normal dinner hour.

"What do you think, Dude? Should I call that uncaring Thomas and give him a piece of my mind?" The cat kneaded my leg and continued to purr. "Yes, I know you like him, and I should trust your judgment, but right now I'm feeling super peeved."

Dude turned a circle, put his front paws on my chest, and rubbed his head under my chin. I softened. We were still into serious woman-to-cat bonding when the phone rang.

"Franklin wants to see us at nine a.m. sharp," Jake announced. "All hell's going to break loose."

My plan was to arrive early Saturday morning and talk to Jake so we could review the nasty encounter and present a united front. He was already sitting at my desk at eight-thirty.

"Franklin's gonna either demote or fire us."

"We didn't do anything wrong. At least not precisely. You were driving too close, and the guy got mad, that's all."

"And he smashed our headlight with a baseball bat. Oh, yeah, that's all. I'll have to walk or take a bus after this." Jake emptied another can of cola and tossed it into the waste basket. "I've been up all night dreading this morning."

We knew it was Franklin when the office door burst open. Without a word, he pointed to a meeting room. Closing the door, he scowled at Jake. "What's your explanation for damaging a state car? This better be damn good."

"We saw the white truck." Jake paced from one corner to the other. "You know, the one that dumped the pig carcasses in the field. Darren told us it was in the Nicollet Avenue area, and we spotted it on our way back."

"How did you know it was the same one? Did you think about it logically? The meat was dumped last week. And did Darren also tell you that his state car was damaged chasing after meat yesterday? After I gave him specific orders, which he dismissed."

"We heard this," I answered, supporting Jake. "But we didn't know he was looking for the truck."

"Makes no difference. His car is damaged; your car is damaged. The commissioner of health will not be pleased.

The taxpayers will not be pleased. What kind of warped reasoning were you using?"

"Not good, sir," Jake conceded.

"I'd say so. If I didn't need you on the salmonella investigation, I'd confine you to the lab washing floors for a month." Then Franklin turned to me. "And you, young lady, had better not engage in any more detective work either. Stick to your jobs, both of you."

"Yes, sir," we replied in unison as Franklin turned and left the room.

"Whew." Jake sighed, sagging into a chair. "It could've been worse."

"Maybe Monday we should just go right to the factory and avoid the office altogether." I offered a temporary escape.

"Agreed on that. But you know if the Gophers win the football game this afternoon, he'll be in a better mood next week." He managed a weak smile.

"Let's hope so. Before you leave, do you have time to compare notes from yesterday? I'd like your opinion about a couple of sanitation logs."

"I've got a few minutes. Meeting some guys for a beer before the game." He grinned and added, "Lucky for us our seats are not anywhere near Franklin."

We went over a few documents and determined specific details to look for Monday. After Jake left for his pregame revelry, I took one more look at the stack of Javier's files. Buried at the bottom was the black ring binder I'd taken from the meat market and had not yet returned to Thomas.

Scanning the pages, I looked for anything out of place. The only pages not inserted in the rings were the truck delivery records, folded haphazardly and shoved into the plastic pocket inside the front cover. I removed these, smoothed them out, and examined the information. Only two days of truck refrigeration temperatures were completed. A third sheet had no entries at all. Maybe the driver thought because it was cold outside, it wasn't necessary to do the paperwork.

As I folded the logs to put back into the binder, I spotted a few hard-to-read names on the back of the third sheet. The list was written in pencil. Each entry had a number after it. The name on the top was Pedro, followed by the number 16. I tried to remember how many boxes of unlabeled chorizo were in Sir Pedro's cooler the day I inspected. There might very well have been sixteen. The entire bottom shelf was stacked with the sausage or whatever it was inside the cardboard boxes.

I was betting Thomas would find this little list interesting.

# 29

Dude was waiting for me at the door, demanding a rub behind his ears and a quick, comforting hug before resuming his cool detachment. I set a bag of groceries on the counter and spotted my cell phone next to an empty coffee cup. Anticipating the meeting with Franklin this morning must have affected my memory.

"How could I forget this?" I mumbled and started to review missed calls and emails. Thomas had called and then texted while I was getting chewed out by Franklin.

He had tried to follow up after the accident after all. So why was I still upset with him? Was it because he only tried twice? Or because he waited over twenty-four hours to call?

"Dude, what should I do about Thomas? Can I trust him? I just don't know what to think."

The cat rubbed against my legs, purring. It was almost time for dinner.

Before he finished inhaling his creamy salmon and chicken, my phone vibrated on the kitchen counter. It was Thomas.

"Yes," I answered, still undecided about my feelings.

"How are you doing?"

"Could be better."

"Want to talk about it?" His concern mollified my apprehensions. "How about I stop over? I can give you a little info about the two we arrested Thursday night. Plus I still owe you pizza."

The cat stood on his back legs and pawed my knees.

"Yeah, it seems the Dude wants to know how soon you'll be here."

"Fifteen minutes."

As soon as Thomas had thrown his coat on a wing chair, Dude pounced on it, rolled around, and proclaimed his satisfaction.

"Have you bribed him? He doesn't like strangers. Do you have catnip in a pocket?"

"Just guy bonding." Thomas sat at the end of the sofa farthest from my chair. "We males stick together."

Before I could think of a starting point for our conversation, he opened the door. "About Thursday night. I intended to drop by later to see how you were doing, but when an officer is involved in an accident with a city plow truck, there's a lot of paperwork. And more paperwork for the arrests. And even more for the shooting. It was well after midnight when I left, too late to call you, Laura."

"A text would have been nice," I reminded him.

"Maybe. But a text is impersonal, and I wanted to see you."

"You texted this morning," I replied, lacking appreciation.

Ignoring my testiness, he continued. "You'd be interested to know that both suspects were interviewed today, and we've been digging into their backgrounds. The snowplow hijacker has an arrest history as a juvenile for selling drugs. Now he'll have assault on his record as well. We still don't have much on the SUV driver. Subpoenas were issued for both suspects' addresses this afternoon, but I haven't heard anything yet."

Dude hit the floor with a thump, sauntered to the sofa, jumped on the cushion next to Thomas, and rolled on his back, anticipating a belly rub. Thomas obliged with a gentle touch, and my dark mood collapsed.

"Something to drink?" I offered.

"Water is good, thank you."

He hesitated taking the glass I offered, looking closer at my face. "How bad is the bruising? I should have sent you to the ER to be checked out."

"Don't be ridiculous. I'm just fine."

"No consequences from the car attack last night?"

"You know already? What? You have spies in the department keeping an eye on me?" I didn't know whether to be annoyed or pleased.

"I saw the report by chance, Laura. No spies, I promise. But it does worry me."

"Honestly, Thomas, I don't know if this had anything at all to do with Javier. The truck driver was not at all pleased to have Jake tailing him."

"The license plate was stolen last week."

"It still doesn't connect to the meat market." I tried to appear unshaken by this information.

He gave me one of those looks that doubted my reasoning abilities, and I changed the subject. "I have some information you might like."

I opened the black three-ring binder and removed the pencil-written list. "Look at these names. The first one is Pedro. That could be Sir Pedro's. The second one is Big Burger Barn on the east side of downtown, and the third one looks like Joe's Market in my district."

Thomas looked at the piece of paper for several seconds. "Where did you find this?"

"In this thing." I handed him the ring binder. "I think it's a list of delivery stops for the suspect boxes of chorizo."

"I'll run this by our drug task force to see if any names sound familiar." He smiled. "Nice detective work."

"Probably my first and last." I told him about our reprimand from Franklin and how Jake and I planned to report to the Baker's Best factory early Monday morning to avoid any additional scolding.

"How about we try pizza again tonight? I promise to turn off my phone, watch out for errant city snowplows, and deliver you safely back to your door."

"You're on, Detective."

Soft snowflakes danced around us when we left the building, twinkling in the city lights. I looked up at the dark sky and let flakes melt on my nose and cheeks, enjoying the quiet elegance of winter.

Thomas opened the car door. I slid inside and waited while he brushed a light layer of snow off the windshield.

"Your unmarked car tonight?" I looked at his dash and auxiliary equipment. "A computer?"

"Yes," he replied and then spent a few minutes describing it before we pulled away from the curb.

"I suppose you can search all kinds of information on this."

"Depends what I need to know."

⌒

The dining room was full, and we waited in a corner of the busy bar for our table to be called. Over our glasses of wine, he asked again, "Are you sure you're okay? Any stiff neck, back pain, deep bruises?"

"To be honest, my ego was bruised when you didn't call the next day. But it's mostly recovered."

Then he switched topics so fast I didn't have time to swallow my chardonnay.

"What happened to your ex?"

I stared at him. "What brought this up?"

Thomas leaned back in his chair and pursed his lips in deliberation. "Well, I've just been thinking about it, that's all. I've seen lives totally destroyed by abuse, and I'm glad you have the strength to come through it. I was wondering if you'd ever reconsider and file charges."

I swirled the wine, sniffed the fragrant liquid twice, and took a very slow, thoughtful mouthful.

"No, I don't ever wish to file charges. I never, ever want to cross his path again. Case closed."

"Okay. Got it. How about those Vikings?"

I laughed. "They may have a chance to be in the Super Bowl in the next ten years."

Smoked pork and roasted red pepper pizza proved to be even better than Thomas had promised. While others around us chatted and laughed and clinked glasses, we ate without conversation, enjoying the food.

Finishing the last piece, I proclaimed, "I'm in love."

His dark eyes sparkled. "With me or the pizza?"

"I don't know much about you, Detective. What are your finer qualities?"

He rested one elbow on the back of the chair and picked up his glass. "Handsome and smart? Those are definitely fine qualities. Currently single and unattached? Maybe those are even finer."

"What does 'currently single' mean? Previously married?"

He took several seconds before answering. "I was engaged four years ago. She decided my work hours didn't meet her ideas for a quality marriage." He went on to explain. "You've already observed this is not a single-shift day job. If we're on a case, I might work twenty hours straight. If we've made an arrest, I might not have a scheduled day off. She couldn't abide the uncertainty."

"I get it," I replied, peering into his black eyes, looking for truthfulness. I wanted to believe him, to trust again.

Neither of us spoke, perhaps contemplating our pasts and the future.

Thomas lifted his glass. "A toast to our evening." The glasses met with a pleasant ping. "May there be others."

Quiet snow was still falling on the drive back to my apartment. The streets were getting icier, and the salt trucks hadn't yet been dispatched. Thomas concentrated on driving, and I opted not to divert his attention. I wondered if I should invite him in or not.

My dilemma was solved when the car pulled to the curb in front of my building. "Night," he said. "Can we try this again?"

# 30

Jake decided it would be smarter to drive his own vehicle than to check out another state car for our trip to Baker's Best factory. I was grateful to climb into the warm interior of his Jeep Cherokee and leave my car parked in the apartment building garage.

"Brrr, it's miserable today," I complained, closing the car door. "Thanks for picking me up."

"Not a problem. Will a cappuccino do?" he asked, handing me the cup with a cardboard sleeve.

"Wonderful. Thank you, Jake. This starts my day right." My hands wrapped around the coffee and luxuriated in the warmth.

"How was the rest of your weekend after the chewing out Saturday morning?"

"Yesterday was relaxing and quiet. How about you?"

"Did a quick run up near Brainerd. Some great trails up there."

I translated this to mean the snowmobiling was good.

He abruptly changed the subject. "Your bruises look a little worse. You okay?"

"Fine, thanks." I sipped the coffee and looked out the side window.

"Who was driving when you had the accident? Did you see a doctor?"

"Of course not. It's simple bruising from the airbag," I answered with a shoulder shrug and studied the coffee cup.

"Was the driver injured?" Jake continued to probe.

"Only his pride, I suspect." My tension level had risen from zero to six.

"The cop, huh? What'd he do, run a red light with his siren blaring?"

I could have given Jake all the details or gloss it over and change the subject. Since it was obvious that Jake didn't like Thomas, the gloss job seemed appropriate. "A snowplow hit our rear end, that's all. Can we just change the subject?"

"Just be careful, Laura. You could do better than a cop."

"What exactly do you mean by that?"

"I just mean, well . . . " He swallowed. "I mean you're educated and have a great future, and he's . . . he's just a cop."

"So you don't think he has any training? Or he's beneath me? Or just what do you mean?"

"Nothing, okay? Nothing. I just don't trust some cops. That's all. Forget it." He turned on the radio, and we listened to jazz for the remainder of the drive.

$$\backsim$$

When George and his inspectors arrived, we gathered in the meeting room for directions. George sat at the head of the table and handed out assignments.

"Before I forget," he added, "Mr. Lundeen, the factory manager, will not be here to assist us today. This, however, will not be a deterrent in our work. The rest of the staff is at our disposal."

George assigned Jake to dig deeper into the lab reports, and part of my responsibility was talking to employees about records. George agreed there were too many questionable entries on logs, as well as missing information.

Food production factories are required to document critical food temperatures, chemical concentrations for sanitizing, and thermometer calibrations, all of these prescribed in their approved food-safety plan. Some data is logged electronically; other information is entered manually. Each manual entry must include the date, time, and employee initials. If the entry doesn't meet food code standards, the employee must take corrective actions and document them. The supervisor or manager must verify that this was done and the information is accurate. It's a whole lot of paperwork.

It's also how the factory proves it's following the law and producing food that's safe to eat. Missing electronic logs, lapses of entries, or erasures on manual logs raise questions and can lead to warning letters, fines, and potential closure by the regulatory authority. Baker's Best's logs had a lot of holes.

George suggested using the break room for my employee interviews. I cleaned the sticky table and two folding chairs before sitting down to review the employee list.

I began with a tall, thin Somali man named Mohammed. He was responsible for cleaning large equipment including the two-hundred-gallon steam kettles for cooking chicken and the room-sized pastry machine that flattened and cut the dough and then pushed it into containers to be filled with potpie mix further down the line.

His forehead scrunched with worry lines, Mohammed asked, "Am I going to be fired?"

"No. No," I tried to reassure him. "There are just a few questions about the work you do."

He nodded and sat down.

"Your job is to clean and sanitize the big pieces of machinery, correct?"

He nodded in agreement without looking directly at me.

"How do you clean the big kettle?"

He fidgeted in his chair. "Sure, sure. I use the green hose and spray inside."

"Only one hose?"

"Oh, yes. That's all I need. The water is very hot," he answered, inspecting his cup of coffee before taking a sip.

I referred to the written operating procedure from the factory manual and showed him the page. "This says you use a hose with hot water and detergent. Does your hose have soap?"

"Oh, no. Just hot water from the hose." He took another swallow, wrinkling his nose at either the hot brew or the question.

"How is equipment washed and sanitized in the pot and pan sinks? Chemical is required for the final rinse." I showed him records where the sanitizer was recorded every day. "Who entered this?" I pointed to the written entry. "Aren't those your initials?"

"Oh, Mr. Lundeen write that. It's his job."

"Mr. Lundeen, the factory manager? He enters your initials?" I put the pen down and looked directly into his eyes.

"Yes," he replied, peering over the rim of the cup, hoping it hadn't been a mistake to tell me.

"So Mr. Lundeen enters this information, even though it wasn't really done?"

"We are told not to touch those papers," Mohammed confirmed, wiping perspiration from his forehead.

I switched to another line of questions. "Can you remember if anybody has been absent with illness this past year? Missing a day or two of work?"

"We always work," he answered, looking at the wall clock.

"Even if you're sick?"

"We don't get money if we're not here," Mohammed asserted, turning in his chair to survey a vending machine.

I thanked him for his time and wrote comprehensive notes before calling in another employee, who cleaned small utensils and equipment. He was also Somali, but his language skills were not nearly as precise. I managed to understand that he also didn't use any chemicals because there weren't any to use.

The small room felt stuffy, overburdened with evidence of mismanagement and outright fraud. A temporary escape was in order. I found clean white jackets hanging in the employee locker room. I put one on, plus a hairnet, and the blue shoe covers employees wore on the production floor.

Similarly dressed, George and his crew were examining a giant steam kettle, using flashlights and taking numerous photos. I watched them for a short time before taking my own unguided tour. The factory floor was poorly lit, a situation that made detail cleaning more difficult. There was also an undefinable odor that gave me an immediate impression of uncleanliness and the beginning of another jarring headache.

Mohammed was pushing a four-tiered cart with dirty bowls and small utensils toward the three-compartment sink. He smiled and called me to the dish room.

"In this sink we wash these," he said, slipping the food-soiled items in the three-foot-by-three-foot sink filled with water. Using a brush, he quickly wiped a large rubber spatula. "Then it goes in here, like this," he explained, dipping the utensil into the second sink and then tossing it onto another transport cart, eliminating a required sanitizing rinse in the empty third sink.

"Is there soap in this sink?" I pointed to the wash water.

"No, Mr. Lundeen says hot water is good enough. We do not waste the soap."

"And this sink?" I swished my hand in the sink he had just used to dip the utensil. "There isn't chemical in here either?"

"Some people say a chemical used to come from this thing here," he said, pointing at the sanitizer dispenser head mounted above the third sink. "But not anymore."

"Mohammed, where are your soaps and cleaning products stored? Can you show me?" I couldn't believe there wasn't any inventory of these critical products.

Mohammed led me down a long, dark hall. Half the overhead lights were burned out, and a few of the remaining fluorescent bulbs were flickering close to extinction. The floor was crusted with salt and sand from the boots of the delivery people and dirty wheels on the delivery carts. I wondered how often these floors were cleaned. Another question for my growing list.

The chemical storage room lacked even the usual products for cleaning floors or a degreaser for tough jobs. Even worse, mouse droppings had accumulated next to the wall where the rodents had established their highway.

"Are there mice in here, Mohammed?"

He scratched his head and pinched his eyes closed, deep in thought. "I don't see one. Maybe."

"This is not good at all. What room is next to this?" I asked, fearing it was bulk food product.

Mohammed took me next door to view the storage of potpie containers and outer packaging. More droppings. Even without using a flashlight, I found mouse urine stains on the storage shelves and saw boxes with chewed holes. Still no traps or bait boxes.

"Is it always like this? Mouse droppings everywhere?"

"Not always," Mohammed assured me with a big smile. "Just since winter came. They want to be warm."

My jaw dropped.

"Are you sick?" He looked concerned.

I shook my head. *But I'm getting there.*

"And where are the dry products stored? The flour, sugar, salt." I could only guess what those spaces looked like. Warmth and food. What more could a decent rodent ask for?

He led me back down the hall into the production area. We walked behind the pastry machine and entered a large room stacked with one-hundred-pound bags of flour, cases of shortening, salt, and other dry ingredients required to produce Baker's Best products.

From the abundance of droppings, it was obvious the mice were much happier here than the chemical storeroom.

"Have you seen mice in here?" I asked Mohammed.

"Not much today. But there were many last week."

"And did anyone come in to trap them?"

"No, miss," he replied, looking a little confused.

Frustrated after that encounter, I sought coffee. Either from a vending machine, which I hoped didn't have mouse contamination inside the working parts, or maybe from a pot of long-simmering brew sitting on a warmer, slowly evaporating into thick caffeine sludge. Strong enough to kill a headache. I headed for the office.

Passing the meeting room, I heard Jake yelling into the phone. "He's left? Do you mean he's on a break or he's gone for the day?" Jake listened. "He gave his notice Friday and didn't come in today. Are you serious? Let me talk to the lab manager or the company president, whoever's available."

While he waited, I quickly related my discoveries.

"Talk to George," he directed, ear still glued to his cell.

# 31

Darren Wolfe decided he would continue the search for uninspected meat, and since Franklin's employees weren't assigned to him today, he'd do it his way. The state car had a new tire, and he was ready to burst into a few more places on the list.

Kyle agreed to ride along with him again. Two other inspectors were more than happy to take the second car and half of the business list. They were familiar with Darren's racist attitudes and frequent rants and were glad to escape his harangues. They wished Kyle the best of luck.

All of them, however, were on the lookout for a small white delivery truck. Darren was absolutely certain it was moving uninspected meat.

"Sure wish these cars had seat heaters," Kyle lamented as he latched his belt.

"State isn't going to be that luxurious." Darren turned the engine key.

"Why don't you use your damn seatbelt?" Kyle complained. "Doesn't that ding, ding, ding drive you nuts? It does me."

"Too confining. And it stops after thirty seconds."

"Thirty seconds too long," Kyle grumbled under his breath.

At their first stop, the two inspectors weren't surprised to learn that word had passed among the markets about the Department of Agriculture raids. When Darren and Kyle entered the dock door at Cesar's Foods, they were met by an English-speaking employee who escorted them to the meat cooler and the display cases. There was nothing to discover. They returned to the car.

"I know they've moved that illegal stuff somewhere!" Darren slammed his fist on the dashboard. "We aren't going to find anything in either Minneapolis or St. Paul." He turned the engine on and thought a moment. "Let's go back to the office and look at the maps. We can use GPS to pinpoint every meat licensee in the state. I want to go south to Dakota and Goodhue counties, where those carcasses were found."

The map revealed six licenses in the southern metro county that warranted their attention. Darren called his team and redirected them to three locations. He and Kyle took the remaining three addresses.

Their first stop was Cannon Falls, a growing rural town south of the metro freeway beltline, where the Mississippi River bends southward, joined by the St. Croix River as it carves its way toward the Gulf of Mexico. The abandoned pork carcasses had been discovered in this farming area last week.

The two inspectors entered through the front door of Casa de Carnicería, walked directly to the meat counter, and showed their badges. Kyle explained the purpose of the visit in Spanish, and he answered questions from the employee.

"Oh, *sí, sí,*" the employee replied, wiping his hands on his bloodstained apron. He opened the cooler door and stood alert as the two men entered.

"Where's he from?" Darren asked Kyle.

"His name is Luis, says he's the manager, and he's from Guatemala. I've gotten to know a few poultry workers who came from that area. Life was tough there."

Two gutted pigs hung from hooks in the meat cooler, both with obvious USDA inspection stamps. Darren inspected the stamps and rubbed his hand over the ink.

"It's legit."

"I'm not surprised. The guy doesn't want to jeopardize his business. He's trying to get his wife and family here."

"You learned all that in a short conversation?" Darren asked.

"I think he wanted to be very clear about his status."

"Ask him if he's heard any rumors about illegal pork deliveries."

Darren watched the two men talk for several minutes. Kyle wrote something on his notepad and showed the employee for his consensus. They shook hands, and Kyle nodded toward the door.

"Well?" Darren asked as Kyle snapped his seatbelt. "What's the scoop?"

"The scoop?" Kyle laughed. "Let's see . . . when is the last time I heard that phrase?"

"Ah, the hell with you. What did he say?"

"He was cautious. He may know something about illegal meat, and he may not. It depends. If he did know something, he suggested looking at a market south of Cannon Falls, closer to Pine Island. It's on our list."

"What did you write down?" Darren started the car engine.

"The address and the name of the manager. He also heard the market had a fire this weekend, so it may not be open at all."

"Time to check it out." Darren turned the car onto the street and drove south.

During the fifteen-minute drive, the two men debated their mission. Darren was positive he'd find more meat to condemn. Kyle was sure the illegal product had already disappeared.

"Look, Darren," he argued, "whoever's behind this knows you're looking. They'll find a different state for the pigs or the drugs or whatever illegal operation this turns out to be. Some other area where there aren't as many inspectors or the locations are remote and only get an inspection every other year. Who knows? But my opinion is this search is at a dead end."

"Let's just see what the next place is like."

Indeed, there had been a recent fire. The market roof was partially collapsed; black sodden timbers crushed the front door and windows. The strong odor of smoke still permeated the air. Darren and Kyle walked around the building, surveying the damage. In the back parking lot, they found the burned shell of a vehicle.

"Maybe this is actually the truck that dumped the carcasses in the field instead of the one we saw yesterday in

town. At any rate, the fire sure destroyed all the evidence."
Kyle kicked a charred piece of metal.

"Can't even find the VIN number on this baby. I wonder
if it was filed off," Darren answered as he tried to scrape off
debris where the vehicle identification number should have
been.

"I'm thinking your investigation died with this fire. This is
not an amateur's game, Darren. The cop was right. Drugs may
be involved. Time to drop it."

# 32

George and his staff were still working in the factory production area, swabbing equipment, floor drains, walls, and refrigeration units. They took fifty swabs last Friday, twelve food samples Saturday, and planned to test another fifty surfaces today. Two coolers filled with samples and paperwork had already been sent to St. Louis via express courier. Two more would be sent tonight.

The noisy dough machine was again in full operation. Shouting over the din, I informed George about the falsified records and the mouse infestation.

"Got any idea how long the records have been doctored?"

"Lots of dates are missing. Jake's running into the same thing with the lab reports. Not only are they missing—no backups can be found at the lab."

"I'd like to shut this place down now," George shouted, "but until our swab tests prove the salmonella came from this factory, all we can do is issue a warning. And we'll definitely investigate that lab. For now, keep digging, Laura. I'd like a smoking gun when it burns their dirty fingers."

Thus, I dug.

My next stop was with the office secretary, who turned out to be the hesitant young woman with the stringy hair we'd met briefly on Friday.

"I'm sorry, I don't remember your name," I apologized.

"It's Sheila. You're with the inspectors, right?"

"Yes, and I'd like to access factory records in Mr. Lundeen's office. Would it be possible to have the door unlocked?"

"We can do that," she decided with a smile. "Certainly you need that information for your investigation." She called for someone to unlock the office door.

The maintenance man was appalled when he entered the office. "Don't usually look like this," he mumbled as he leaned over and gathered papers. "Waste basket not even been emptied."

Curious, I asked, "How does it normally look?"

"Better'n this. Looks like he threw papers everywhere. Leastwise there was always space on his desk. This here looks like somebody trashed it."

The large desk and worktable were covered with sloppy stacks of papers and manila folders. Loose pages littered the floor. Three shelves of the bookcase were jammed with unlabeled binders, and a tower of well-used eighteen-by-eighteen-inch boxes teetered in a corner.

"Just leave it for now," I told him.

He nodded and left, closing the door to hide the chaotic mess from coworkers who might think he hadn't done his job.

Where to start? Looking for the easiest task, I began with the piles on the desk, scanning the pages in each folder to get a general idea of the subject and labeling it with a sticky note to describe it.

It was tedious, the kind of work that fosters a headache and an unnatural desire to escape for a walk in the snow. Even cold, biting northwest wind seemed preferable to this jumbled mess.

Within an hour, I had cleared space on a side worktable and started new, neater stacks that stood erect. Close to noon, Jake stopped in to drop off a sandwich in a triangular-shaped plastic container and an apple that had become old and wrinkled in the vending machine waiting for someone to purchase it.

"The expiration date was two days ago," I complained.

"You're most welcome."

"I'm sorry. Yes, thank you for bringing lunch, however old and expired it may be."

"You're having a challenging day too, I see," Jake sympathized. "How goes the scavenger hunt?"

"Slowly and curiously. How about you?"

"Frustrating. See you at five."

The turkey and cheese on whole wheat was dry and uninspiring, much like the paper shuffling. It was obvious that some daily logs from the past year had been recently completed and backdated six to eight months. The paper was smooth and clean, and the entries were all done in the same color ink. Older legitimate-appearing documents were smudged with fingerprints and smeared ballpoint. I knew I was looking at counterfeit records.

Most of the phony documents were records for chemical sanitizing, which wasn't surprising. But there were other suspicious entries and omissions that were puzzling. Why were some records for the cooler temperatures missing? Maybe they would eventually show up in the paper jungle. I opened Michael's computer, looking for a digital data logger app. Loggers are used to record temperatures in refrigerators or in delivery vehicles or used in hot prepared food to track cooking and cooling times. I assumed the missing records would be in these files.

Sheila couldn't help me with the password. I asked about tech support. Could they access just the specific files? She didn't know but would be most happy to find out and get back to me.

Her helpfulness both amused and puzzled me. Why the hundred-and-eighty-degree change in attitude from Friday? How did the introverted and unhelpful secretary become assertive and resourceful overnight? I was tempted to ask outright but decided on a wait-and-see approach.

By late afternoon, both daylight and my brain were fading. I'd shifted documents into logical files, identified each binder on the shelves, and cleared the desk. There had not been time to sift through the boxes in the corner. I anticipated that privilege would be passed to someone else tomorrow.

On second thought, maybe another day in the potpie factory wouldn't be too bad. The Gophers had not won their football game on Saturday, and Franklin was probably still fuming over the broken headlight on the state car. Staying out of the office one more day might be a blessing, even if it meant reading boxes and boxes of records.

In the end, it wasn't my choice. Before we left for the evening, George announced he'd just been informed that six swabs from last Friday were positive for salmonella and were undergoing advanced DNA testing to determine if it was the same species that already killed two people. And since so many issues with records and personnel had already been uncovered, we'd all return in the morning. In addition, top management from Ohio was flying in, and he wanted each of us to summarize and present our findings. George was hoping for more final lab reports before the meeting so he could officially close the factory.

Jake exploded as soon as we climbed into the cold car. His hot tirade fogged the windows, and after suggesting twice that he turn on the defrosters, I finally did it myself.

"Lundeen and the lab tech have to be in collusion. I'd bet on it. Missing records, incomplete records, inaccuracies. If our lab sent reports like that, the director would be fired. I'm not even sure this place has a director. For sure we want to know who else uses their services—if you can call it a service." He raged on. "I've never seen such incompetence. What I don't understand is who's gaining what here. Lundeen is hiding contaminated product. Okay. So he has his job to keep. But why would the lab tech send false reports? What's he gaining?"

"I'd guess a bribe, Jake. Which is why neither of them was at work today."

"That's possible. If the tech is getting bribe money to send false reports or to lose them, he stands to gain. Assume Lundeen is paying out. He's just trying to save his job. But depending on how big the bribe is, isn't he losing money in the long run?"

"I've been thinking about that as well. All the faked records are curious. Maybe he's not just a salaried employee. Maybe he's part of the ownership. More profits to share. I'll talk to Sheila tomorrow."

# 33

Jake dropped me at the curb, and I hurried inside to escape the descending darkness and chill of November. All I wanted tonight was some hot soup and a good book for total distraction.

I pulled a container of chicken soup from the freezer and nuked it for five minutes. I'd made it two weeks ago and froze enough for three more bowls of comfort on cold, snowy nights like this one.

The book was a new work of fiction by an Australian author I wanted to try, and the cat on my lap was a no-brainer. Dude was ecstatic.

I forgot to mute the cell phone.

"You're not calling from the lobby, are you?" I asked Thomas.

"No. I'm still at my desk. Looking at pictures, as a matter of fact."

"Of your last vacation?" I teased, rubbing the cat behind his ears.

"I wish. No, these are from a security camera two buildings

down from Javier's market. The system wasn't registered with the city, so we didn't know about it. One of our investigators found it this morning."

"And?"

"And there are some questions you may be able to answer when you look at these," Thomas replied.

"Not tonight," I protested before he even asked. "It's been a long day, and I'm definitely not going back out into the cold. Dude and I are quite content to read my book."

"Dude reads?"

"Very funny. Seriously, Thomas, I'm not going anywhere tonight."

"How about tomorrow after work?" he offered. "Drop by my office to take a look at these pictures, and then we can catch some phô and spring rolls."

"It'll be closer to six. I'll be back at the factory one more day."

"Okay, maybe I'll bring the photos to you. Catch up with you tomorrow."

I poured a glass of red wine and returned to the book. The phone rang again. The number was familiar. I debated.

"Yes?" I answered cautiously.

"This is Dorothy. Do you remember me? Dorothy Martin. My husband died from the bad food."

"Yes, of course I remember you."

"A man called to say he'll sue the food company for me. He's a lawyer, and he wants all the records. Can you help me with that?"

"Who is he?" I wondered how someone had gotten her

confidential contact information this early in our investigation. "He needs to be qualified to represent you. He should understand the mechanics of foodborne illness."

"Oh, let me see," she said. "Just a minute."

I could hear rustling in the background before she returned with the information. "Brandon Becker. Is he any good?"

"What is he promising to do, Dorothy?"

"Get me money, of course. And he'll handle it all afterward too. He has a service for that."

Big and small alarm bells pounded a warning. "Wait, Dorothy. Do not sign with him yet. I'll do some checking tomorrow. Where did he get your contact information?"

"He just called me tonight. He can get money for me," she repeated.

"Dorothy, why don't you call the county senior advocate? They'd find out if this lawyer is a scammer or not. Or call AARP. They might also be able to help."

"I don't need a senior advocate or the association for retired people. I'm fine." Dorothy cut me off.

# 34

Before morning coffee, I contacted the police department, asking for their senior citizen fraud investigator. The call went to voicemail, but I left a detailed message about Dorothy and the suspicious attorney Brandon Becker.

Next was a call to Franklin's voicemail. "How did an attorney named Brandon Becker get Dorothy Martin's contact information? The official investigation into the death of her husband is ongoing. Nothing's supposed to be available to the public until we complete our inquiry. Please call me. Oh, and I'll be at the factory one more day."

In spite of the bone-chilling wind, I was still incensed when Jake picked me up a little after 7 a.m. "She's a vulnerable old woman. He'll just take her money and run. I bet he's a total sleaze ball."

"Maybe she sought him out instead of the other way around," Jake suggested.

"It seems unlikely. How would she do that? I don't think she even knows how to use a computer."

"Look, Laura, you offered help; she refused. Let the police look into this. You've done all you can. Let it go."

"Easier said than done." I stared out the window at the heavy gray clouds that threatened more snow.

George and the three other inspectors were already there. Sheila brought a coffee pot and a box of doughnuts to the meeting room.

"Thought you all might want a little something for your meeting with the big guys from Cleveland. They're coming on the company plane this morning and should arrive by ten. 'Bout time they got their butts up here." She smiled and closed the door.

"Do I sense a certain joy in Sheila this morning?" an inspector observed.

"Seems like it," George replied. "Michael Lundeen will not be joining us again. That might be the reason. And I've ordered all production stopped until after the management meeting.

"Laura, I want you to continue talking with as many employees as possible. Try to get a broader picture of what's going on. Do the employees see mouse droppings in the steam kettles in the mornings? Or on the dough belt?" He took a long swallow of coffee. "What training did new employees have when they started working? See if you can find training records, pest control contracts, documents like those.

"Jake, there are boxes of files in Lundeen's office. Pull anything that appears falsified, is unsigned, or is otherwise questionable. Make copies for our evidence files.

"You two," he said, pointing at his colleagues, "are going to tear apart the dough machine piece by piece looking for mice nests. I think we can show the management team what's happening. They'll have to issue a recall for everything produced here in the past two to three months at least. We want no arguments from them."

Jake's phone rang, and he ducked into the hall to answer while George fielded questions.

A minute later, he returned. "Good news. Our lab found salmonella in three of the frozen pies purchased yesterday. One with an expiration date of next month, so it's been on the market awhile. Maybe the recall will extend to six months of production."

"I'll drink to that," George said, lifting his cup. "Now let's get to work and finish this up today."

I entered Sheila's office and asked, "Can you provide training records and pest control documents? And George wants every single employee interviewed. I'll need a list."

"I can get that info for you in a few minutes. Do you want attendance history? I can supply it as well. You might find it very interesting."

"You are definitely in a happy mood today, Sheila."

"You betcha I am. The sooner Michael Lundeen is gone, the better. Since he arrived, morale has been horrible, turnover even worse, and accounting says profits are down. You wanna know why?" She didn't wait for my answer.

"Because he's a thief, and a couple of the men he hired are too. Maybe into drugs too—I don't know for sure. Notice how all three of them were out yesterday and today? It's because they know what's coming down.

"Those big shots from Ohio should have been here long before this," she continued. "Wanna know what I think?

Michael lied on his quarterly reports. Among other things he lied about."

"Why do you think he's into drugs, Sheila?"

"His eyes were always dilated, that's why. And he sniffs a lot, like someone who snorts coke," she answered.

"You don't like him much, do you?"

"Nobody likes him. We lost some good, experienced people because Michael let them go and hired ones who still can't do a decent job, if they even show up to work. Can you believe he comes in here and tries to tell me my job? I can smell his cheap cologne two minutes before he gets here. Gives me time to disappear."

After she finished her tirade, I asked, "Did Michael order the chemicals for cleaning and sanitizing?"

"I don't know. You can ask our accountant. Come on, I'll take you to his office. You two can talk while I pull up the other info."

She led me down the hall to another office, knocked, and entered. "John, this lady is part of the investigation, and she wants to see chemical invoices. Can you help her?"

"Yeah, sure." He swiveled in his chair to open a file drawer. "Most of our chemicals come from Pilot. Usage has gone up significantly in the past six months. Expensive stuff. Affects the bottom line."

"You're sure use has gone up?"

"Yes, especially that quaternary stuff, whatever it is. They must be drinking it at breaks."

"Quat is a chemical sanitizer," I clarified. "And your inventory is zero."

"Can't be. We've ordered cases of it."

"May I look at the Pilot invoices for this time period?"

"Yeah, sure. Give me a couple of minutes. I'll make copies for you," he replied.

As I waited for the invoice copies, my phone rang. "Ag and DEA found traces of cocaine and marijuana on the dumped carcasses," Franklin announced. "It's now officially a case for the feds. The police are done with the investigation at Sir Pedro's. Use common sense when the place reopens. If it doesn't feel right, leave it alone and get out. I want two people in the place for inspections from now on.

"And in regard to the lawyer who contacted Dorothy Martin, I double checked with everyone, including the interns. No one has received a request for information about the investigation or about Jim Martin. Maybe her friends are the source. I've never heard of the lawyer either. Advise Mrs. Martin to be cautious."

"I did try to warn Dorothy, but she's in a vulnerable state, Franklin. In my brief visit, I witnessed verbal abuse and indicators of other deprivation. She won't take help. That's why this lawyer thing is strange."

Franklin sighed. "I know you won't stay away from this."

"Here you are." The accountant handed me a thick pile of invoices when I put my phone in my pocket. "Good luck."

As I walked past Michael Lundeen's office, Jake called out, "Get a look at this." He'd opened several boxes from the precarious corner stack and removed the contents. "Some of these documents don't even have a year on them. Is this a report from June sixth this year, last year, or three years ago?" Smoke was almost coming out of his ears.

"You'll probably have to look through all these boxes to figure it out."

"Yeah, well, I'm tempted to take every one of these things to Lundeen's house and ask him what the hell was on his mind when he filed them without a complete date. Or better yet, find the lab tech who ran the tests in the first place."

"Why don't I take this stack to Sheila to make copies for George while you keep looking? She's in such a good mood today, she'd probably copy all those boxes for us."

Indeed, she was happy to oblige. "No problem. Bring it all in, and I'll get the job done. And please let everyone know the Ohio big shots will be late. Their flight has been delayed another hour due to heavy snow in Cleveland. They won't get here until noon."

# 35

Darren was not pleased. "So I'm supposed to just stop tracking the carcasses? You think the cops can do it better?" He drummed his fingers on the desktop. He was tempted to hang up.

"It's a drug case. The meat is no longer in the food supply. Let this go," Franklin advised.

"But we're so close. Yesterday we found an incinerated meat market and truck south of Cannon Falls. I think it was Javier's truck."

"Did you notify the police?"

"Nah, not yet."

"Stop now, Darren, before you get in over your head. Are you going to call the police," Franklin demanded, "or am I?"

"What's the cop's number?"

Franklin recited the phone number and added, "Right now, Darren. Not in ten minutes."

"Damn," he sputtered, ending Franklin's call. "Cops don't know a thing about tracebacks. Inept idiots."

Darren picked up his half-filled cup of coffee, took the elevator down one floor, and entered the blueprint storage room. It took forty minutes to find the plans. His hunch about the burned market was correct.

He punched Kyle's number on his cell. "Where are you? On your way home already?"

"I'm monitoring the roads southwest of the cities. The winds are gusting over thirty miles an hour, and it looks like the State Patrol might close the highways around Marshall and Redwood Falls due to drifting snow. Guess I'll stay until it blows through. What do you need?"

"I've been thinking about the Mexican guy you talked to at the Cannon Falls market. Do you have an impression he wasn't telling us everything?"

"Guatemalan," Kyle corrected. "Yeah, it's possible he wasn't entirely upfront. I know he was very careful with his answers."

"If we talked to him again in strict confidence, is it possible he might tell us more?"

"What's on your mind, Darren?"

"I'm looking at the blueprints for the burned market. It was a big operation with four large walk-in coolers. It had to be a distribution center. I'm betting those carcasses in Javier's came from there. And I think the unmarked truck was the delivery vehicle. I'm betting our butcher friend can fill in a few details."

"Shouldn't this be a job for the cops?" Kyle asked.

"They don't know anything about tracebacks," Darren barked. "I don't believe the drugs are related to the pork. Those were added later, probably by Javier."

Kyle was silent.

"Look, all I want to do is talk to the guy, okay? But I need you for translation. And I don't want to call him because he'll just hang up. Are you with me or not?"

"I suppose. You'll go on your own anyway and get into trouble. I'll come along to keep the translation as clear as possible."

# 36

A small group of idled employees sat around the breakroom lunch table drinking cans of pop or coffee, voicing confusion and indignation about the abrupt halt in production ordered by George. I pulled out an empty chair and joined them.

"What's going on?" Mohammed asked. "Will we be paid for today?"

"Where's Lundeen? He'd fix this," an employee complained.

"I'm gonna sue you if I lose my job," another threatened.

"You've all seen the mice. They live in the dough machine, and their turds can end up in the potpies. Did you think this was normal?" A calmer voice from the burly man at the end of the table silenced the hostility. He stood and braced his muscled arms on the table, staring down complainers. "Let's give this lady a chance to explain," he insisted.

"Thank you." I nodded in appreciation. "To the point, the reason production has been halted is because of the mice and because we can now prove the potpies have not only made people sick but are also responsible for at least two deaths."

"Not true," came an angry denial.

"It's been confirmed by lab tests," I replied. "Your product is contaminated with salmonella, most likely from the mice running amok in the whole factory. Do you see mouse traps anywhere? Who does pest control here?"

"Don't know," the dough maker replied, "but they don't do a very good job. Lundeen finally got motivated a couple days ago and gave us some overtime to clean up. Said we're getting an inspection of some sort. I guess this is it, huh?"

"Yes. This is it."

"Well, do we just punch out for today, or what are we supposed to do? What do I say to my wife?" moaned another, with his head in his hands.

"Management from Ohio is arriving shortly," I advised. "They'll make these decisions."

When I left the employee break room, I spotted the Pilot Chemical deliveryman pushing a dolly piled with cardboard cases. "Good morning," I said and introduced myself. "Is this a normal delivery?"

"Yeah, it is these days. They use a hell of a lot of chemicals. More'n any other place I deliver to. Twelve cases of sanitizer today. Business must be really good."

"Who usually signs for the delivery?" I asked.

"Ah, it's usually Lundeen. If he's around. Makes no difference to me as long as somebody signs off."

"What's the billing for this delivery?"

"Well, this here delivery of four cases is over three thousand dollars. That ain't countin' the other stuff I still hafta unload. You know, soap and degreaser, stuff like that." He pulled a sheet off his clipboard. "This here's the invoice. Looks like close to four grand in stuff today."

"Is there a black market for these chemicals? Is it possible someone could sell them for more than this?"

"Maybe," the driver considered. "Lundeen gets the top bulk discount. I s'pose he could sell it full price to some little guys and pick up extra cash for the company. Never heard of it, though," he added.

*Better yet,* I thought, *if Baker's Best paid for the chemicals, Michael Lundeen could sell them for less than the normal delivery price and pocket all the money.* I thanked the Pilot employee for his help and headed up the stairs to review the chemical invoices provided by the accountant.

Jake and George were bent over a laptop, discussing mice.

"See here?" George pointed. "There's a dead mouse on that ledge. It's been there so long it's desiccated. And look at this," he continued, moving to another photo. "See all the droppings under the dough machine? They've been living off the scraps that fall on the floor and are never swept. It's not hard to see how the potpies were contaminated." He was scrolling for another photo when two agitated men in heavy overcoats threw open the meeting room door.

"I'm Jack Takano, VP of operations, and I want to know exactly what's going on here." He jerked his wool muffler off, pulled off his black wool coat, and threw both on a vacant chair. "We were contacted yesterday and told it was a critical situation. It damn well better be."

"Miserable flight," the other muttered under his breath, removing his gloves.

"Well," George replied calmly, leaning back into his chair, "we knew you'd want to preside over the temporary closing of this factory due to unsanitary conditions. Care for a donut?" he asked with a mischievous smile.

"Where's Lundeen?" the VP asked, scanning the room. "Where the hell is Lundeen?"

"Michael Lundeen is not here today," George answered. "If you'd both care to take a seat, I'll get the rest of my staff, and we'll detail the reasons for closure. You may find this enlightening."

Jake and I exchanged raised eyebrows and suppressed smiles.

In a weak attempt to take over the meeting, the VP rolled his chair next to George and flung open his briefcase to cover some of the official paperwork.

George pushed it aside. The VP glared.

"I wouldn't tangle with George if I were him," Jake muttered.

Two inspectors came up from the production floor for the meeting. George introduced his staff and handed the VP a folder. "Why don't we start with the document on the top? The lab reports detailing the DNA match of the salmonella bacteria found in your potpies and also from the stools of people who ate them."

The VP leaned back in his chair and looked around the table. "Why isn't Michael Lundeen here?" he asked again.

"I advise you to read the report conclusions describing the type of salmonella and the genome sequencing."

"What exactly is genome sequencing?" The VP sounded peeved.

"WGS, or whole genome sequencing, details the DNA

patterns of bacteria that cause foodborne illness. When two patterns match, we know the pathogen is from the same source. I could provide a half-hour tutorial, but now is not the time," George added. "The next page identifies salmonella from our swabs taken on the dough belt and inside the feeder hose for the potpie mix in this factory. It's exactly the same DNA as the species cultured from the two men who died."

George paused to let the information sink in. The VP turned white.

"Additionally," he continued, "we have preliminary reports of salmonella in Baker's Best potpies purchased at a local grocery last Friday. One of the packages has an expiration date of March next year."

"I told you there was something shifty about Lundeen," complained the second executive. "His reports just didn't add up. Can we sue him?"

"Ask our attorney. Right now we've got bigger problems. If this factory will be out of production until it can reopen, we need to gear up the Indiana factory to cover the output. Call them and tell them to offer twelve-hour shifts with overtime pay."

George pushed his chair back, stood, and leaned over the table, pressing his hands on the top. "Gentlemen," he announced in a firm voice. "We are here to discuss the issues in this location. The Indiana factory will be getting an inspection very shortly to reassure the USDA that operation is in total compliance and the food it produces will not make the public ill. Now put away your cell phones, get out your legal pads, and take notes while we review our findings."

Jake and I started the round-table discussion with our

investigation into the deaths of Jim Martin and Arthur Kruger. We explained the chain of custody procedure used to collect the potpie samples and produced a copy of the paperwork documenting the temperature of the product at the time we collected it and at the time it was received by the lab.

"We should've brought our lawyer along," the VP grumbled. "Can we challenge this?"

"Don't think so," Jake replied.

George's investigator described how swabs were taken, secured, and sent to the government lab in St. Louis. "Not likely you can challenge this process either. Look at the photos of the mouse turds and chew holes. Our attorneys have enough evidence right now to take you to court."

"Not to mention logs that appear to be falsified or undated," Jake inserted.

"We don't think you want to challenge anything," George advised. "Of course, you have the option, if that's what you think you want to do. For now, let's draw up a plan of action to recall all products made in this factory, for a professional cleaning of the equipment and infrastructure, and for staff training. We're not leaving this room until we finish."

Jake motioned, and we slipped out the door. "I want to talk to Lundeen about these lab reports this afternoon. Before he skips town."

"Let it go, Jake. This place is closed. Let the feds inspect the cheaters at his lab."

"You coming along or not?"

"Just pick me up at four-thirty. And try to keep your temper in check," I called as he barreled down the hall.

# 37

"You're driving too fast," Kyle warned. "There are icy patches on the road."

"Okay, okay." Darren slowed the car by a couple miles per hour. "I just want to talk to the little weasel and find out what he really knows. None of this *no sé* business this time. Got that, Kyle?"

"What the hell is your problem? Aside from being racist?"

"He lied. And you know it." Darren ignored the accusation.

"I don't think he's involved," Kyle answered, "but I'm sure he knows there will be severe consequences if he supplies names."

"What do you mean *severe*? We find the illegal slaughterhouse and close it down. He pays a fine. End of story."

Kyle exploded. "How can you be such a single-minded ass? There are drugs involved, Darren. Drug dealers with guns. Do you really think he'd risk his life to help you find your uninspected carcasses? I don't think so. But I'll certainly ask him if that will satisfy you."

Light snow was falling when they parked in front of the

market. Neither had spoken in the last thirty minutes. Darren exited the car and slammed his door, stomping through the soft white flakes like a scolded child. Kyle waited until he entered the market door before following.

Waiting at the meat counter, Darren tapped his fingers on the glass case. "All I want is the supplier. I don't give a damn about any drugs. Just the meat supplier. Can you do that?"

"I can try. Keep your mouth shut," Kyle ordered. "And stay here."

He found Luis on the loading dock, checking in deliveries of pig and beef carcasses. Instinctively, he looked for the purple ink stamps on the animal hides that assure inspection. Each carcass was properly marked.

"*Hola. Tengo más preguntas.*" ("Hello. I have more questions.")

"I very busy now. No have time." Luis continued counting boxes and checking the invoice. "All meat is inspected, see?"

Showing no intention of leaving, Kyle stood and watched. Six minutes passed, and he saw Darren standing just inside the swinging door, angrily eyeing the standoff. Kyle glared back, and Darren retreated.

Kyle watched Luis move to a darkened back corner and pull out his cell phone.

"Come on. Get with it. I gotta get moving," the delivery truck driver announced. "The snow is gonna set back my schedule. Sign this thing so I can leave," he demanded, approaching Luis.

Completing his conversation, Luis hurried to sign the invoice and pull down the overhead dock door after the driver left. "Come to my office." He motioned to Kyle.

The room was small and stuffy and overheated. Luis closed the door and sank into a well-used chair, wiping his sweaty forehead with his shirtsleeve.

"Look, man, this is not good stuff. You no want to be involved. These are really bad guys."

"We aren't interested in the drugs. We just want to know where the pork was processed. Just tell me if it was here in Minnesota, yes or no?"

Luis paused to consider the request. "Not here. Texas."

"That's all I need to know. It's out of our jurisdiction. As far as I'm concerned, we're finished with this investigation."

Luis nodded in agreement. "Watch your *amigo*," he warned. "He's going to cause trouble."

"I'll take care of him." At least Kyle hoped he could.

"Drive careful, my friend. The highways are slippery. Use the county road; it was just sanded."

Where was Darren? Kyle had expected to find him waiting outside the office door. He looked down two short grocery aisles. No Darren. *Now what's he gotten into? Another one of his righteous confrontations?* He walked to the meat counter. Only a lone woman in a puffy down jacket stood in front of the refrigerated case, pointing to her intended purchase.

Kyle was turning to leave when he saw Darren emerge from the meat-cutting room.

"I got some information that might help us," Darren proclaimed with a big smile. "I probably did better than you did with slimy Luis."

"Let's just get out of here. Tell me in the car." Kyle didn't even want to talk to him. And he was feeling anxious about the building storm.

The two men trudged across the parking lot, now white with over an inch of swirling fluffy snow. The wind had picked up, carrying white flakes from the northwest and reducing visibility.

"You drive," Darren ordered, handing over the keys. "I don't like driving in snow."

"Yeah, thanks. The roads are going to be miserable." Kyle turned the ignition key. "Buckle up."

Ignoring Kyle's request, Darren asked, "What did you learn?"

"Carcasses were from Texas. Not our jurisdiction. I'm done with this, Darren."

"Did you check the stamps on the carcasses he just received? Did you write down the processor number?"

"No, Darren. They were legit. He'd be really stupid not to get inspected meat right now. He's not dumb."

"Well, somebody is a liar, that's for sure. Luis says the meat is from Texas; the butcher said the pork came from Colorado. I don't believe Luis for a second."

"You believe what and who you *want* to believe. That's your problem, Darren."

"I've been in this business enough years to know when someone is lying," Darren countered. "And Luis is not telling us the truth."

"Look at it this way. Either the pork carcasses came from Texas or from Colorado. Not our territory, not our problem. It belongs to the feds. Period. End of investigation."

"Maybe," Darren muttered.

The center line of the highway disappeared under a coat of white, forcing Kyle to slow his speed. "It'll take us an extra hour to get back to the office. This is why I wasn't driving home today, but now I'm stuck in it anyway. Storm wasn't supposed to hit the metro area."

"This is not exactly metro," Darren replied. "Maybe we should stop somewhere until it blows over. If this car gets damaged, I'm in deep trouble with the fleet guys."

"Oh, yeah, the slashed tire. It was a warning to stay away, but here we are, mucking around in this case anyway."

His speedometer read forty-five miles per hour, and Kyle considered slowing down even more when a silver pickup truck emerged from the whirling snow behind them.

"He's going too fast," Kyle yelled. "He's gonna hit us."

The pickup moved into the passing lane and pulled even with Kyle. Then the truck swerved into the state car, brushing the driver's door.

"What the hell is he doing?" Kyle took his foot off the gas pedal to fall behind.

The truck also slowed down, keeping an even pace with the car. It swerved again, hitting the car with more force. Kyle slammed on his brakes and pulled the steering wheel to the right into an uncontrollable spin. The car slid off the road, went down an embankment, and rolled.

Snow continued to fall, covering the tire tracks.

# 38

After Jake left, I searched for the employee who wasn't afraid to speak up about mice, the big man who lifted heavy stainless mixing bowls and dumped the forty-five pounds of pie crust mix into the rolling machine. I found him zipping his gray winter jacket, preparing to leave.

"Not going to stay around to find out what the plan will be for reopening?"

"Nah, they'll have to change a lot of things here before I'd come back. I'll find work somewhere else. And it won't be overrun with mice, and it will have better management."

"Why haven't you left before this?"

"I liked the hours. Working during the day instead of nightshift. The pay was decent. But when Lundeen came on, it all changed. How he could let the mice run like that—I didn't get it. And we all knew he was stealing chemicals."

"Did you ever figure out why he stole them?"

"Never looked into it. Didn't want to get fired. Doesn't look good on a job app."

"Anything else we should look at? Something that might help our investigation?"

He scratched his head, looked to one side, and looked back at me. "Check the freezer records. Unit wasn't working for three days last month."

"Thanks," I called out as he made his final exit.

Sheila had given me copies of the refrigeration logs that morning. I should have looked at those before George's meeting, but it wasn't too late to do it now. Because most of the factory employees had left, the break room was empty. I wiped a table with a napkin to remove the sticky remnants of spilled sugar and coffee creamer before spreading out the papers.

The electronic dated logs and graphs were easy to interpret. It would have been impossible not to see the two days of temperatures above seventy degrees in the freezers. The out-of-control readings were printed in red. I guessed the thawed potpies were not destroyed, just left to refreeze and shipped to customers. That would explain a potential for growth of salmonella. Even a few bacteria would have multiplied significantly in a couple of days.

As I gathered the papers for George, my phone vibrated. I recognized the number.

"Hello, Dorothy."

"My lawyer still doesn't have the information he needs," she complained. "He really wants it now so he can start the paperwork."

"We're not done with the investigation. Until all the reports are finished and verified, nothing is available. Is there some reason he can't wait?"

"I want my money. Now."

"Do you know who recommended him? How did he find you, Dorothy?"

"He said he knows Rose and Peter Born. Does that satisfy you? Well, I can see you're not going to help me at all." Bang. Call over.

At the time of the interviews, I thought the Borns were well-informed people who wouldn't even know a shady lawyer, much less recommend one to a vulnerable widow. I still thought this and wanted to verify it. But first I needed to get the temperature logs to George.

I cracked open the meeting room door and saw Sheila taking notes as the group around the table listened to one of the USDA inspectors. George motioned for me to enter. I placed the incriminating documents in front of him, pointing to the red-lined charts and the dates.

"Gentlemen," he announced, "these records document two days of incubation temperatures for the potpies. No records of product disposal. Our attorneys will find this illuminating. Time to put your recall plan into full action."

"Right now?" sputtered the VP.

"Immediately," George responded. "Everything since this date." He pointed to the temperature logs. "Everything shipped since September thirteenth."

"Nice detective work," he whispered as I turned to leave.

Next on my list was contacting Peter and Rose Born about the questionable lawyer talking to Dorothy.

"Why, no, we didn't refer anybody to her," Peter replied to my question. "Never heard of the guy. What's his name again?"

"Brandon Becker."

"Let me ask Rose. Maybe she knows about this. Rose!" he yelled into the phone, forgetting to hold it aside. "Rose, did you call Dorothy Martin about a lawyer?"

Rose took over before my ears started to ring.

"No, I didn't say anything to Dorothy. I wonder where she got that idea? She actually said we recommended him?"

"Yes, he told Dorothy he knew you. Rose, I know how interested you and Peter have been about this entire process of investigation. Who else would you have shared this with?"

"Well, ah, Peter told the guys at the VFW."

"What about social media?" I asked. "Facebook accounts, tweets, things like that?"

"Honey, I couldn't tweet if I was a starving robin." Rose giggled. "But I do have a few friends on Facebook, and I may have mentioned what happened."

*Yes, I bet you may have.* "How many friends do you think you have, Rose?"

"Oh, maybe . . . let me think." She paused. "With the kids and the grandkids and the church friends and the card groups, and a few others, of course, maybe sixty or more."

I did a quick calculation. Their version of the illness story posted and reposted could have easily topped several hundred, if not more. And who knows how many people heard the story from Peter and repeated it?

"Okay." I sighed. "Would you please call Dorothy and reassure her you don't know this guy, you never recommended him, and suggest she seek legitimate counsel?"

"Yes, of course," Rose affirmed. "Peter can help her."

"A warning to you. She's furious with me for suggesting

legal aid or any other assistance. She may be resistant to any advice you offer."

"Peter is charming," Rose asserted, "and persuasive. He'll handle it."

My next call was to Franklin, updating him on both the findings here in the factory and Dorothy's situation.

"How soon will the recall be announced?" he asked.

"Within the hour. George is insistent."

"Good. I'll get the staff out checking grocery stores tomorrow. You're done there today, correct?"

"Yes. George and his crew are finishing this afternoon. They'll handle the paperwork. As soon as Jake returns, we're heading back."

"Where is Jake?"

"He took some records to Lundeen's house to ask about some entries."

"Remind me again, who is Lundeen?"

"He is, or rather was, the plant manager. He may be indicted after this investigation."

"And Jake couldn't let the feds handle it? No, of course not," Franklin answered his own question.

"At least he's not chasing white delivery trucks," I tried to joke.

Franklin changed the subject. "Did Darren tell either of you about finding the burned truck chassis in Dakota County?"

"No. Unless he told Jake."

"Hmmm. I'll have to have a little talk with Darren about this," he said before ending the call.

I decided to take a last look through the boxes of files in

Lundeen's office. George already had enough information to justify closing the facility and issuing a recall. But I wondered what else might be hidden in the mess. Jake hadn't opened several boxes. I had time to tear open a few more.

Two U-Haul boxes anchored another six we hadn't looked through. Curiosity directed me to those two on the bottom. Unlike other boxes, these were taped shut. The first one was filled with personal papers and a photo album.

From the look of the hairstyles, I'd discovered a collection of photos taken during the 1970s. Under the album was a death certificate for someone named James Russell and more photos. The second box was mostly books and still another collection of photos. Nothing was related to the factory operation, and I wondered if these had been stored here and forgotten by some manager in the past.

Pushing those aside, I opened another carton and found papers pertinent to the factory.

"Find anything of interest?" George asked, entering the office.

"Other than undated records with missing information, not much."

"Don't worry about it. We'll subpoena all this. We're going to hit the road in an hour. Our flight is scheduled to leave at nine tonight. By the looks of the snow, it may take us that long to get to the airport. You and Jake should get going too."

"I'm waiting for Jake to return. He decided to speak directly with Michael Lundeen about the records."

"Not really necessary," George said. "But I do like his spirit. Thanks for all your help. And please tell Franklin I owe him one."

By four-thirty, I was tired of sifting through boxes and was beginning to worry about Jake. I tried his cell phone, but he didn't answer. I hoped no answer meant he was driving and on his way.

As I put the phone back into my purse, it rang. Aha. It had to be Jake.

It was Thomas. "Can I drop over with these pictures in an hour?"

"I don't know if I'll be home by then. Jake was supposed to come back and pick me up, but he still hasn't shown. I'm beginning to wonder if he's slid into a ditch."

"You're still at the factory?"

"Yes, and everybody is leaving soon because the factory is closing."

"Any security personnel?"

"There was one, but he may be going too."

"Find someone to wait with you. I'm on my way."

"But what about Jake?" Dead air. "Well, damn it." I tossed the phone back into my purse.

Sheila entered the office holding a sheaf of papers. She laid them on the desk and asked, "Problems?"

"I don't know if Jake forgot to come back, or if he's been in an accident, or if he's still talking to Michael Lundeen. He doesn't answer his phone. Someone else is coming to pick me up, but that may take an hour."

"No worries. I'll be in the office with the VP. He's reviewing all the feds' documents and our shipping statements for the past three months. We'll be here awhile. Enjoy the coffee."

Grateful someone would remain in the building, I opened another cardboard carton.

# 39

Jake's head throbbed; he opened his eyes, felt his world spin, and quickly closed them. Through the pain, he tried to remember where he was. He was cold, lying in complete darkness, hard concrete underneath his aching body. Slowly, he reached to touch his left temple and felt a large, tender protrusion he judged to be the size of a baseball. *What the hell happened?*

He recalled Sheila giving him Michael Lundeen's address. Not exactly outright because it broke too many company privacy rules. Instead, she made the information available by leaving a paper on her desk with the house number and street.

"I'm going for a powder," she announced.

From where he had stood in her office doorway, it was five short steps to her desk. He copied the address into his phone map app without ever touching the paper. Easy enough. Even with light snow on the freeway, Jake had figured he had plenty of time to confront the factory manager with the damaging documents and return to pick up Laura by four-thirty.

The more he thought about the meeting, the tighter he'd gripped the steering wheel. He would ask, *Don't you care that two people already have died due to your malfeasance?* Would the man sneer at the accusation, or would he take responsibility?

*Should I punch him in the jaw just for the heck of it?* Jake had seethed, pushing the gas pedal a little harder.

The address was easy to find in an older neighborhood of the southwest metro area, not far from the bustle of Excelsior Boulevard. He had parked and checked his watch. Not quite two-thirty.

No one had answered the doorbell. Jake pounded on the locked storm door. After waiting for what seemed like five minutes, he'd walked to the back.

He had the same lack of response to his persistent pounding. As he'd turned to leave, he glanced at the single-car garage. The side door stood slightly ajar.

"Anybody here?" Jake had called, entering the garage. That was the last thing he could remember.

How long had he been lying here? He lifted his arm, squinting to check the time. After four-thirty. How would Laura get home?

# 40

"Anything from Jake?" Thomas asked when I slid into his car.

"Nothing."

"Might he have contacted Franklin?"

"That's possible, I suppose. Although he's driving his own car, so if he's in a ditch, it's not likely he'd call the office. But I'll check." Thomas was merging into I-494 traffic when Franklin answered.

"Have you heard from Jake?"

"No. What's he done now?"

"He was supposed to come back to the factory an hour ago. Thomas drove out here to pick me up."

"This makes two missing persons tonight. I had a call from Kyle's wife wondering what delayed his drive home. She hasn't heard from him for over six hours."

"Has anyone checked with Darren? Maybe they're together," I suggested, hitting the speaker button so Thomas could hear the conversation.

"Speaking of Darren." Franklin sounded annoyed. "Did he call Thomas about the burned vehicle?"

Suddenly, the car ahead of us fishtailed into the left lane. I grabbed the door strap to brace myself. Thomas pressed on the pedal, and our antilock brakes kept us aligned as the car slowed.

"No call from Darren," Thomas answered as if nothing had happened. "What vehicle was he describing?"

"Damn it. The one behind the burned meat market south of Cannon Falls. He and Kyle found it when they were trying to trace those carcasses. I told him it was police business."

"Have you tried calling Darren?" I asked again.

"Haven't had time to think about it. We're swamped with illness complaints. In fact, I could use your help."

"Tonight? Really, Franklin? Have you looked out the window?"

"I need a full team, Laura. How long would it take you to get here?"

"At least two hours," Thomas interrupted. "And I need her first to review some photos from Javier's."

"Early tomorrow then," Franklin conceded and ended the call.

"Call Darren," Thomas directed me.

Scrolling my contact list, I found his number and tapped the call button. It rang five times and went to voicemail. I left an urgent message to call back.

Thomas called dispatch. "Ask the DTF if they have any information on a recently burned meat market in Goodhue or Olmstead County, somewhere near Cannon Falls."

"Can you be more specific?"

"Best I can do. Tell them it's possibly related to Javier's market."

"DTF?" I asked when he finished.

"Drug Task Force. They're looking at Javier's contacts, cell records, bank accounts, travel. They've found a number of calls to and from disposable phones."

"Maybe there were some to the burned market?"

"We'll look at those," Thomas acknowledged. "Do you think Darren would drive out there again just to look at ashes?"

"Yeah, he's not easily dissuaded when he thinks he's right. I'd guess he had a hunch about something and was following up."

"Not very smart," Thomas concluded.

"So," I thought aloud, "can I sum this up to assume somewhere between here and most likely Mexico, drugs were stuffed into pig carcasses, shipped to Minnesota, and perhaps distributed through the now burned down market near Cannon Falls using the also recently charred van? Javier received these in his Minneapolis market and distributed the drugs to other dealers or directly to customers. But something went wrong, and he was killed, followed by the murder of the manager of Sir Pedro's, which is also on Javier's delivery list. Suspects unknown at this time."

"I'd say you've summed it up," Thomas affirmed.

"I don't understand how Javier got involved in this. He had a growing business, was liked in the community. How does he get into drug distribution?"

"Money. Lots of money."

"But the risks are so great. It cost him everything."

"All relationships have an element of risk," Thomas replied, still looking straight ahead, monitoring traffic.

It took me a full minute to realize our conversation had

changed direction. I stared out the window into the darkness, seeing only headlights blurred by snow and brake lights warning of danger.

"I don't know, Thomas." I twisted uncomfortably and readjusted my seatbelt strap.

"You don't know I'd like to see you more often, or you don't know if I'll even ask?"

"You know what I mean."

"I know nothing," he answered, "but I'm still waiting to hear a yes."

"Yes, with conditions." *What would they be? Do I even know?*

He turned to look at me. "And those are?"

"We start from chapter one in the dating manual," I replied, attempting to lighten the mood.

"There's a dating manual?" His eyes were back on the road.

"I'm writing it," I replied with a silly grin. *Whew.*

"Will I get an autographed copy?" He was more serious than I expected.

"Of course you will."

"Works for me," he answered and reached to touch my hand.

"Both hands on the steering wheel," I ordered, seeing the car ahead hitting the brakes.

"Yes, ma'am."

We drove in silence, Thomas watching the traffic creeping ahead of him while I kept an eye on cars attempting to merge into our lane. I felt relieved yet cautious about the road our relationship would take.

"Try calling Jake again," the cop Thomas ordered. "Then try Darren. Was either one of them driving a state car?"

"Jake was in his own vehicle this morning," I confirmed. "And I assume Darren and Kyle used a state car. I'll check with fleet services."

"While you make the calls, I'll get Jake's car info." Thomas pulled off the freeway and parked in a back corner of a busy fast-food parking lot. On his computer, he found the vehicle information for Jake and notified the State Patrol.

I punched in the number for the office of state fleet services. It was still open, but the clerk was unable to tell me which car Darren had been allotted. "We close in twenty minutes, and I won't be able to get the information until tomorrow."

Thomas grabbed my cell. "This is Detective Thomas Garcia of the Minneapolis Police Department. There's reason to believe Darren is in a dangerous situation, and we need to find him now, not tomorrow morning. Let me talk to your supervisor."

It was amazing how fast his attitude changed with the right motivation. We had the car make and license within three minutes. Thomas radioed these details to both Cannon Falls Police and the Goodhue County sheriff before pulling back into traffic.

"We should be at your place in fifteen minutes. Does shrimp and noodles sound good? I'll drop you off so the Dude can be fed and keep me in his good graces while I pick up a couple cartons from Quang Restaurant. We can look at the photos while we're eating."

"No wonder Dude likes you." I laughed.

"Sometimes I think he likes me better than you do."

"I'm not sure what you mean." I swallowed a lump of doubt.

"Yes, you do, Laura. What are you afraid of? Was your marriage so horrible that you're afraid to trust again?"

"I told you." I felt defensive. "He was abusive. Isn't that enough information?"

"But you didn't know it going into the relationship, did you? He turned into Mr. Hyde soon after the wedding, I'd guess. And you're wary of me because my first marriage was canceled before it happened, and you're wondering what I did to destroy the relationship. Isn't this what you're thinking?"

He was still staring straight ahead, monitoring traffic as if nothing had been discussed, as if my angst had not been attacked.

"Yes, damn it, that's right. I'm afraid you'll turn out to be a lying drunk who lashes out with his fists every time something doesn't please him. I'm afraid of having my self-esteem pulverized again."

"I can promise you none of that will ever happen."

"I've heard promises like that before."

"I'm sure you did. Still, you're willing to take a chance on me as long as I adhere to the dating manual. You write it, and I'll abide by the rules. Will this work for you?"

"You're willing to do this? Why?"

"Because I've met a beautiful, intelligent, kind woman who loves her cat. And I like her cat too." He smiled without looking my way. "Six blocks to your apartment," he announced.

# 41

I almost tripped over Dude as he wound around my legs on my way to the kitchen. I knew darn well it wasn't me he was so thrilled to see; rather, it was the anticipation of being fed within the next three minutes.

His bowl filled, I turned on the oven, poured a glass of wine, and sank into the womb of my wing chair.

*What have I done? For six years, I've studiously guarded myself from being hurt, avoided close friendships with men, afraid of where they might lead. Now I'm committing to a dating manual? What was I thinking? I'm not ready. Will I ever be ready? What will happen if Thomas gets angry? Will he react with a fist?* I shuddered.

Dude hopped on my lap, licked my hand, and curled into me. His purring soothed my jumbled thoughts.

*I'll take it slow. I'll be aware of even small signs of uncontrolled anger. Thomas is patient, not harsh. He has a dry sense of humor that makes me laugh. Even his eyes smile. He's not pushing me into something I can't handle. I'll give him and myself a chance.*

Within twenty minutes, Thomas was back with the food.

He popped it into the oven while I pulled two plates and another wine glass from the cabinet. Dude wound around his legs just as he had mine.

"You've been fed, you beggar," I admonished.

"Can't blame the guy for trying." Thomas laughed and poured wine into his glass. He proposed a toast. "To the dating manual."

I smiled as our glasses met with a reassuring ring.

When his phone rang, Thomas walked into the living room to answer. I put plates on the table, eavesdropping.

"No one? No tracks in the snow? Nothing? Have the hospitals been checked?" He listened. "Yeah, yeah, I know it's a crazy night and all your units are out and the ambulances are busy, but find someone to check. They were picked up and left somewhere," he added.

"Not good," he said before I could ask. "They found Kyle and Darren's car rolled over in a ditch along Highway 149. It was empty, and they couldn't find any tracks of the two men, which is not surprising since it's been snowing for over three hours and visibility is poor. They may have wandered into the fields or have been picked up by someone. Police are checking hospitals as they have time."

"Can they tell what happened to the car? Any blood?" I held my breath, expecting the worst news.

"If you mean evidence of violence, no, there wasn't any. There was blood on the seats, and the windshield was impacted on the passenger side, consistent in a situation where someone wasn't wearing a seatbelt."

"How soon before we learn more?"

"Could be a while. As he told me twice, they're

overwhelmed with accident calls." He sniffed. "I smell shrimp."

We'd barely begun eating when his phone rang again. It was the Drug Task Force guys. This time, he put it on speaker.

"Thanks for the tip on the Cannon Falls market," the voice offered. "Ownership papers are murky. Four owners, no licensed vehicles listed. We're now checking the licenses of other meat markets in the county."

"Was Javier the sole owner of his place?" Thomas asked.

"Yeah, he was," the voice answered.

I interrupted. "Any link to Sir Pedro's? I do recall a change of ownership about six months ago."

"We looked at that but couldn't find any tie-in," the voice replied.

"Thanks for the help," Thomas acknowledged before he ended the conversation.

"Why didn't you tell them about Jake?"

"There isn't any connection." He shrugged.

"That doesn't give me comfort. Maybe I should start calling hospitals."

"If you know where Jake went, we can guess a route and contact possible emergency rooms." He opened the takeout bag and placed wrapped chopsticks next to each plate.

"He went to Michael Lundeen's house. I have no idea where it is."

"Why don't you start with Bethany Hospital? I'm going to my car for those photos for you to look at, and I'll check car registrations for Lundeen's address."

On hold with the hospital, I turned on the TV to monitor the news, which tonight was all about the weather. The State

Patrol already reported over two hundred accidents on metro freeways. This number didn't even include fender benders or worse on city streets. If Jake was in an accident, he could still be waiting to have his car towed. But then he should have— would have—called.

The ER receptionist at Bethany didn't think anyone named Jake Schaffner had been admitted. But, she confirmed, their computer was running a little slow from the rush of intakes, and I was advised to call back after 9 p.m.

Thomas had scary news. Michael Lundeen didn't hold a driver's license or have a vehicle license plate in Minnesota.

"That can't be right," I protested. "How does he get to work?"

"If he just moved here from another state, he may not have changed registrations yet," Thomas reasoned. "Is there anyone at the factory we can contact to get his home address?"

"The plant is closing. No one's there."

"Someone was there when I picked you up. Maybe they're still working on the closure plan," he pointed out.

"Sheila might be," I replied, rummaging through my briefcase for her information. I punched her number into the cell phone.

It rang six times before I was relieved to hear her voice.

"Sure, it's right here on my desk." Sheila read the address for Michael Lundeen. "Good thing you called now. I was just on my way out. The recall for the potpies has been posted, and they'll be hiring new management and—"

"Thanks, Sheila," I interrupted. "I'll talk to you tomorrow."

Thomas looked at the address. "He'd have taken Flying Cloud Drive to 494 and exited here," he concluded, pointing at a map he'd brought from the car. "If he was taken to an ER, it would be Bethany. He's not there. I have a bulletin out for his car. All we can do is wait."

"Can't the police do a welfare check or something like that? Or at least drive past the address to look for Jake's car?"

"I'll give them a call, but no promises. It's still most likely he slid off the road or had an accident."

"But Jake is missing," I argued.

"For less than eight hours. He's not a missing person yet," Thomas reminded me.

"Let's eat." He used a fork to pull out what were now lukewarm noodles and shrimp from the carryout container. "And take a look at these photos."

He laid a series of grainy black-and-white security camera photos on the table showing the parking lot and dumpster behind Javier's Market. The first photo, taken at 8:14 p.m., showed a man walking across the parking lot, his face hidden in shadows. The next photo, taken at 8:32 p.m., was of the same person walking back toward the alley. Photo three was clearly Javier following the visitor.

The last series of photos showed both men in an apparent struggle. Javier was knocked to the ground; he rose to one knee; he was on the ground again; the visitor was standing, pointing the gun at Javier. In the last photo, Javier's lifeless body lay in the deserted parking lot. The assailant's hat was knocked off during the struggle, his hair and face exposed to the camera.

"I've never seen this guy before," I reacted, shaking my head.

Thomas pulled another set of photos and laid them out. "Do you recognize this man? He's in photos from Sir Pedro's and Javier's. He drops off cartons frequently, always after six o'clock. That's outside of normal delivery hours, wouldn't you say?"

Not waiting for my reply, he continued, "We haven't been able to identify him. We don't know if he might be a dealer or a user or into something else suspicious. He shows up in several pictures from the last two months' archives."

"That's Michael Lundeen," I confirmed, almost choking on a cold shrimp. "He's been stealing cleaning chemicals from the factory. It looks like you found a couple of his customers."

Thomas was quiet as he carefully looked at the photos. "I don't like the coincidence," he announced. "We need to find Jake. Now."

He grabbed his coat and was almost out the door before I snatched mine from the closet.

"I'm coming along."

"No, you are not," the detective replied.

"The heck I'm not. Jake is a colleague. I'm coming. It's chapter one in the damn dating manual."

He paused at the door and glared.

I glared back.

"Backseat," he ordered.

I didn't say another word until Thomas finished radioing for assistance and we sped along the snowy streets to the freeway, red lights flashing as we passed through intersections of stopped cars.

His radio interrupted my thoughts. The Hopkins police were two blocks from the Lundeen address.

"Use extreme caution," he warned. "The guy may have a gun, and it could be a hostage situation."

"What's your ETA?" the radio voice asked.

"Ten minutes or less."

Maybe Jake wasn't there; maybe he was in a car accident and wasn't able to call. Maybe his cell phone was damaged in the accident, and he couldn't call. Maybe, maybe, maybe.

We arrived exactly eight minutes later. "Stay here," Thomas ordered as he exited the car and drew his weapon.

I watched him confer with other officers before they approached the house. I got out of the police car and crunched through new snow to the opposite side of the street, where I could watch and listen as the police entered. My body shivered from tension and cold wind. The cops breached the front door.

Windows of curious neighbors lit up, casting a warm yellow glow on the sparkling purity of new snow. Peeking through drapes and blinds, they watched the drama continue on their quiet street.

An ambulance stood sentry at the end of the block, waiting for a casualty, the EMTs nearby, blowing their cupped hands for warmth. Police cars blocked both ends of the street, denying access and escape. How long would this take?

Lights clicked on systematically in the house, room by room, as each was searched. Heavily armed cops stood watch in front, waiting. Suddenly a voice called from behind the house, "He's in the garage. Get the medics here, stat."

Was the *he* Jake or Michael? Was he alive or a still body? I crossed the street and stood in front of the adjacent house, listening and hoping to hear Jake's cocky voice asking for a diet cola.

Lights flashed as the ambulance stopped in front of the house. The paramedics raced up the driveway with their gear. I edged closer, but an officer ordered me to return to my house immediately.

"I came in that unmarked car," I said, pointing across the street.

"Then get back in it," he ordered.

"Can you just tell me who they found?" I pleaded. "I work with Jake. I need to know if it's him and if he's still alive."

"Look, ma'am," he offered with detectible compassion, "wait near the ambulance."

"Thank you," I whispered.

It seemed like forever before the paramedics came back with the gurney. They returned with Jake, oxygen mask clamped on his face, lying deathly still, pale as snow.

"Jake." I touched his arm. "Jake." A swollen eye fluttered.

Thomas put a hand on my back. "You're not in the car, I see."

I swung around, expecting anger and a stern lecture, only to be pardoned with an approving nod.

"Ride to the hospital and stay until I get there. When he comes around, ask him what happened."

# 42

Thirty minutes later, an ER receptionist took me back to Jake's treatment area. Two IV bags hung from a metal stand, a heart monitor pinged nearby, and a large bandage covered the left side of his head.

"Jake," I whispered.

"I'm here," he answered without opening his eyes.

"Do you remember what happened?"

"Don't know for sure. Happened too fast."

A nurse entered carrying a warmed blanket. "Good thing you weren't out there any longer," she commented before leaving. "You'd have frozen to death."

"Now that was a pleasant observation," he mumbled. "What time is it?"

"Almost ten. You've been here over an hour. Shall I call someone for you?"

"No," he murmured and drifted away.

I followed the bed as orderlies moved him to a third-floor room, and I waited in the hall for the neurologist to finish his evaluation. Franklin exited the elevator as the white-jacketed doctor came out of Jake's room.

"How's my epidemiologist doing?" he asked.

"Assuming the swelling recedes, we'll do an MRI in the morning to determine if there's internal damage. At any rate, he's going to have one big headache for a few days." The doc tilted his head back, staring at the large man who'd asked the question.

"Aren't you Franklin Hamilton? Played for the U about eight years ago?"

"Yes, I am," Franklin confirmed with a big smile.

"Wow. You were awesome. I remember when you were drafted. How long did you play?"

"Less than a year with Houston. Did a number on my knee. The pros can be a short career. You were wise to choose medicine," he told the young doctor before walking into Jake's room.

Franklin stood at the end of the bed. "How you doing?"

"Could be better. I hurt. Worse than a hangover."

Everything was white and sterile. The sheets, the walls, the blanket, Jake's chalky face, the big bandage covering his temple and upper cheek. Cold piercing lights, snow hitting the window. I took a deep, numbing breath and asked again, "Jake, can you remember anything from this afternoon?"

"Don't think Lundeen was there. Nobody answered the doors. Garage door open. Can't remember," he answered, eyes still closed.

Franklin nodded at me. "We'll check with you later. Rest now."

Thomas met us in the hall, and we retreated to a quiet table in the family waiting room. Sagging into a side chair, he, too, looked exhausted. "Does Jake remember anything?"

"The only thing he said was Lundeen wasn't there."

"Well, somebody was certainly there," Thomas confirmed, "swinging the shovel that hit him and then replacing it on the storage rack in the garage."

"Would you care to update me?" Franklin demanded.

Thomas spent the next ten minutes detailing the last three days, including my photo identification of Michael Lundeen entering both Javier's and Sir Pedro's. "We're looking for him, and for now, that's all we can do."

"How do Darren and Kyle fit into this? They haven't turned up yet tonight, and I've had a distraught wife calling every hour for information I don't have." Franklin rubbed his brow in frustration.

"I wish I knew," Thomas admitted.

"What role did Michael Lundeen play in all of this?" I asked. "He presumably sold stolen chemicals to Javier, Sir Pedro's, and who knows how many other restaurants. He neglected the production at the factory, resulting in a huge foodborne outbreak with deaths. But this doesn't explain why he tried to kill Jake. Stealing chemicals is one thing, but murder? Was he involved with the drugs? There are a lot of loose ends here, Thomas."

"We'll pull them together," he promised.

"I'll stop back here in the morning," Franklin announced, rising from his chair. "Now I'm heading home. I need you tomorrow bright and early, Laura. The potpie recall is spurring a lot of phone calls."

⌐

It was midnight when we sat down again to eat, opening

a bag of burgers and hot fries. Dude hopped on a chair, whiskers trembling with anticipation.

"You've been fed, guy. Remember? And you batted those boxes of noodles on the floor and ate a few while we were gone. Bad cat," I scolded as if he understood or even cared. "Now get down." Thomas picked him up and put him on the floor.

"He's not going to like you for this," I warned. "Even though you did feed him tonight. Nine lives and nine RAMs of memory, especially when it comes to food."

"I believe you said he was fickle," Thomas reminded me. "He'll get over it."

"Or he'll just ignore you."

"As long as you don't ignore me, I'll be fine." He slid two fries through catsup.

"Why would I ignore you?" I took a big bite of burger to avoid saying more.

"Maybe not exactly ignore, just shut me out. You're still running from intimacy, Laura. I can feel the tension when I simply touch your hand. You tighten up; you pull away emotionally."

I tried to justify my reactions. "I told you what my ex was like."

"Yes, and I remember saying I'm not anything like him."

Familiar hot tears burned my eyes. "No, you aren't." I attempted to smile.

"Good. Now that it's settled, let's finish these burgers before they get cold."

# 43

Dude walked on my stomach, kneading, purring, kneading some more. After jerking out of a nightmare, gasping for air, I was grateful for the reassurance of the cat now rubbing his head on my forehead. How long would these ugly dreams go on?

The luminous clock numbers read 5:45. I slid cautiously out of bed, searching the cold floor with my toes for slippers before venturing into the kitchen. Dude curled up in the warm blankets, in no hurry to rise and shine in the winter darkness. I wasn't exactly thrilled to be up this early either, but somebody had to bring home the cat food.

My cell rang before the water ran through the coffee grounds.

"Good morning, Franklin," I answered as cheerily as possible before my morning caffeine.

Without any greeting, he got to the point. "I stopped to check on Jake, and he's still resting. The nurse said his vitals were good."

I looked at my watch. Six fifteen and Franklin had already been to the hospital. When did he sleep?

"And," he continued, "Kyle's wife called me. He and Darren are in the Mayo Hospital in Rochester. How they got there is still a mystery. Kyle has a broken collarbone, and Darren has head injuries. Apparently he wasn't wearing his seatbelt. Kyle's wife said he now believes the Cannon Falls meat market is connected to Javier's, and he wants to talk to the police. I've called Thomas."

"And what did Thomas say?" I put a slice of bread in the toaster.

"When I woke him, he was pretty groggy."

Smiling to myself, I replied, "Gee, Franklin, what time did you call? Five?"

"I apologized for waking him."

Good thing he couldn't see my eyes rolling. "I'll be in the office in forty-five minutes. How many complaints from the potpies do you have so far?"

"As of nine last night, we have forty-two in Minnesota, plus the CDC has another fifty-two from other states. The number could change after we check the voicemails this morning. I want you to work with the interviewers on the phones. We have a grad student who can do Jake's work part time for now. But he has finals coming up, and his help is limited."

"Will George issue the final report for the factory? Or do we also need our own summary?" I poured a glass of orange juice.

"They're slow getting to those things," Franklin conceded. "I want a detailed report from you and Jake asap."

"See you soon," I said, ending the call. My mind was dizzy thinking about the time and statistical analysis required to do the report. Jake needed to recover in a hurry.

Before I even finished my first cup of coffee, the phone rang again.

"Good morning, Thomas."

"I'm assuming you've had a predawn call from your boss."

"And I heard you did too."

"Uh-huh," he grumbled. "What's your impression of Kyle? Do you think he's believable?"

"I don't know him well enough to give you an answer, Thomas."

"I'd like you to come along to the hospital in Rochester for the interview later this afternoon. Think that would be possible?"

"Why me?"

"Because you understand the business better than I do," he confessed. "If there are inconsistencies in some of Kyle's statements, you'll catch them sooner."

"What time?" I asked, refilling my cup.

"How about three o'clock? Or four?"

"Make it four if Franklin okays it. We have a pile of complaints and an even bigger pile of paperwork."

"Then you'll need a break by late afternoon. A quick road trip should do the trick. And Franklin owes me one for that pre-five a.m. call. I'll be there at four."

⌒

Indeed, a stack of illness complaints filled the epidemiology inbox, though not all seemed to be associated with the potpies. After I did a quick review of the forms, several illnesses appeared to be from norovirus, in particular six unrelated persons with diarrhea who ate at the same Minneapolis skyway restaurant in the past week. These were assigned to two grad students for the follow-up interviews.

I focused on the cases with either acknowledged consumption of the potpies or of clinic and hospital lab confirmations for the same salmonella species. With the local news release announcing the recall and temporary factory closure, the public was now aware of the potential danger.

Each interview took about twenty minutes. The first call went to an elderly man in Duluth. His clinic sent salmonella isolated from his stools to our state lab for further testing. The DNA matched.

Before I could get to the questions, Mr. Novak spent several minutes describing how ill he had been. He finally recalled eating a potpie the previous week but had no idea how long he had heated it. He didn't want to burn his tongue.

I talked to a panicked young mother whose four-year-old was hospitalized with severe diarrhea. Yes, the child ate potpies. At least two last week. It was his favorite lunch. What should she have done differently?

Two college students called the foodborne illness hotline to report they were ill three weeks ago and they missed classes for two days due to diarrhea. They might have had a temperature too. They were never going to eat potpies again.

Before tackling the next call, I joined the conversation at the coffee pot. The grad students were sure they'd determined the food most likely associated with the norovirus outbreak and were comparing notes. All the ill people had at least tasted or eaten pumpkin cookies, a popular item during Thanksgiving month. The cookies came from a Washington County bakery, and according to an initial contact with the manager, his staff baked and frosted about one hundred dozen cookies every other day for local distribution.

Franklin ordered an immediate inspection of the bakery. The sick people had been asked to supply a stool sample. Our interns would drop off specimen cups and pick them up to facilitate the lab work and confirm the virus DNA. They would interview all the bakery staff to determine how many employees were or had been ill. If ill employees were working, the bakery would be closed for thorough cleaning and sanitizing.

Back at my desk, I punched in the number for Jake's hospital room and was pleased when he not only answered but also sounded like he was recovering.

"We miss your expertise here," I consoled him. "Franklin has a student entering data, but he has a learning curve to conquer, and the going is slow."

"I'll be in tomorrow. Had an MRI early this morning, and if it reads okay, I'm outta here. In fact, maybe I should stop in this afternoon."

"Tomorrow will be fine, Jake. Don't rush it. Aren't you under some kind of concussion protocol?"

"Now you sound like Franklin." He changed the subject. "Have they found Lundeen yet?"

"I haven't heard anything. Except he may not really be Michael Lundeen. The state doesn't have a driver's license or a car license under that name."

"How'd you find that out?" Jake asked and then answered his own question. "From the cop."

"The cop is the reason you didn't freeze to death on the garage floor, Jake." I was getting tired of his biting comments and was feeling defensive. "We called Sheila for the address as soon as Thomas realized there weren't any official records for Michael Lundeen. And," I continued before he could reply, "Darren and Kyle are in a Mayo hospital in Rochester. They had a car accident last night. Kyle thinks maybe a market near Cannon Falls is linked to Javier and the drugs. Thomas and I are going to talk with them later this afternoon."

"Why are you going? Can't he do it by himself?"

"My expertise." I wanted to gloat but assumed this was enough for Jake to handle for the time being.

"Yeah, well, just be careful he doesn't get you involved in something dangerous."

"He won't. See you tomorrow."

Thomas called before I could start another interview. "Michael Lundeen is really Michael Russell. His fingerprints were all over the house. Did time in Iowa for grand theft while working for a hotel chain. He stole the same kind of stuff: chemicals, liquor, small appliances. At least now we know who we're looking for."

"I wonder what else he took from Baker's Best."

"Their accountants will figure it out. I don't expect any legit business will call us to say they purchased goods from him, so we may never know the full details."

"What about Jake's injuries?"

"No witnesses. Next time he gets hot under the collar, tell him to slow down and cool off."

"Oh, sure, like he'd listen to me."

"Can you leave at three-thirty? I'll pick you up at the Health Department. We'll get your car later."

# 44

The Rochester Mayo Clinic campus was enormous. The primary hospital, St. Mary's, has over twelve thousand beds, and the receptionist's directions could have used more specifics as to precisely which set of elevators to use. Early-winter darkness had descended when we exited on the eleventh floor and walked into Kyle's room.

For the second time in twenty-four hours, I found myself visiting a colleague in the hospital. My knees felt weak, and my shoulders ached from the muscle spasm sprinting down my back. Leaning against the wall, I attempted a solicitous half-smile as Kyle raised the bed to see us better.

Thomas introduced himself, sat in the only chair, and opened a notepad.

"Thanks for coming, Laura," Kyle directed my way.

"How serious is it?" I asked, looking at his right arm supported by a sling.

"Four to eight weeks recovery. That pretty much covers Thanksgiving and Christmas. Haven't had the holidays off for ten years. It'll be a treat." He winced.

"Pain?"

"Nothing I can't manage," he added, shifting a pillow with his good arm. "But this isn't why you're here." He looked at Thomas.

"First, tell me how you got here."

Kyle closed his eyes to visualize the scene. "After we rolled, it took me a while to get out of my seatbelt. I yelled at Darren for help, but he didn't answer, and I was worried he was dead. As soon as my belt released, I knew something was wrong with my arm. It was really painful. I tried to find my cell phone, but stuff was strewn all over, and I didn't see it. A big guy suddenly appeared at the car door, and it scared the hell out of me. I thought he was there to finish us both off.

"Turned out he was a local farmer. He helped me get out and then pulled Darren out. Darren was awake but really groggy. The farmer helped me up the hill first, and he called nine-one-one, but they said it might be an hour before they could respond. All the emergency vehicles were out, and traveling was slow. So the farmer—I told you he was a big guy, didn't I?—went back down the hill and helped Darren up and then drove us to St. Mary's. And here we are." He took a deep breath and settled into his pillow.

Thomas nodded. "Glad you're safe, Kyle. Your wife called Franklin this morning saying you were certain the meat market was involved in drugs. Why do you think so?"

Kyle began with their first trip to the market in Cannon Falls and then driving to the second market, finding it burned to the ground, and discovering the charred truck. Darren was positive the vehicle hulk was the same one used to move the illegal meat.

"Darren was also sure the market manager was lying,

even though he didn't understand my conversations with Luis. But Darren never trusted anyone, so it wasn't a big deal. I thought we had good rapport," Kyle continued. "I speak decent Spanish; Luis seemed to be above board. He told us about the burned market. His carcasses were all stamped. Why shouldn't I trust him?"

"What changed?" Thomas asked.

"First of all, I really didn't want to drive back down there yesterday. Darren was the one pushing to go. I was monitoring the storm and realized the roads around Marshall would be closed, and I knew I wouldn't make it home. At the time, the storm track didn't include the Twin Cities, so then I figured, *why not?*

"Anyway, when we got there yesterday, it was different. I felt uneasy. Something changed. Luis was unwelcoming, distant. In so many words, he warned me to stay away, to not get involved, as he put it."

Thomas lifted his pen. "A warning is not a chargeable offense, Kyle."

"I'm fully aware of that, Detective. But there's more. Because it was already snowing and blowing, he suggested a highway he was sure would be plowed and salted. And," he paused for effect, "the silver pickup truck that forced us off the road was the same one I saw parked behind the market."

"How can you be so sure? Did you recognize the driver?" Thomas asked.

"I play a little game with my kids when we take road trips. We try to create a memorable description or phrase for the letters on a license plate. I saw VWZ on the truck plate and thought of very wild zebras. When the truck first pulled behind me and tailgated, I could read the W and the Z on the plate."

"But not the letter V," Thomas confirmed.

"No, I didn't see a V. It was snowing, and visibility sucked. But how often do those two letters appear together on a license plate? At least it's worth checking, isn't it?"

"But you didn't actually see the driver either." Thomas sat back in the chair. "What else made you feel something wasn't right?"

"The whole atmosphere had changed in twenty-four hours. Luis went from reasonably cooperative one day to uncommunicative the next. Right after I arrived, he moved away and made a call. I couldn't understand the conversation because he turned his back to me. He ignored me while he checked in an order. And then the warning to get out of this investigation." Kyle shifted in his hospital bed.

"Plus, someone lied. Either he did, or his butcher did. Luis told me their meat came from Texas. I looked at the stamp, and the numbers were familiar, but I didn't verify it. The butcher told Darren it came from Colorado, and Darren said the stamps had been trimmed off the meat in the cutting room."

"Could the butcher be mistaken?" Thomas asked.

"Not likely. You agree, Laura?"

"It's not my area of expertise, Kyle, but I tend to agree with you. In general, a business purchases from the same suppliers because they've worked with them for a significant time and they trust them."

"Yeah, well, there's not a lot of trust in any of this."

"What does Darren think?" Thomas continued.

"Darren thinks everyone is lying until it can be proven otherwise. We don't agree very often, but this time I think he's right."

"How is Darren?" I asked.

"Not great. The idiot doesn't like seatbelts."

"I'd like to get back to your original point," Thomas redirected. "You think drugs are involved. From everything you've said here, I don't see it."

"The delivery Luis was checking in. Boxes and boxes of sausage casings. More than any meat market could possibly use in a year. Unless they would be stuffed with something else."

"Like drugs," I suggested.

"Yeah, after all this, it's what I was thinking," Kyle concluded.

Our second stop was Darren's room.

"Doc said it's a good thing I have a hard head, or I'd have had brain damage," Darren mumbled. Both eyes were black; a line of stitches extended from his hairline to the bridge of his nose. His arm was wrapped in a blue fiberglass cast up to his elbow.

Pointing to the cast, I asked, "What happened?"

"Broken wrist. Fractured ulna or whatever that bone is called. Have two new screws in my arm. Gonna be a while before I get back to work."

Thomas pulled up a chair and retrieved his notebook. "What do you remember about the accident?"

"Little SOB Luis ran us off the road," Darren asserted.

"So you recognized the driver?"

"Had to be Luis. The guy was lying the whole time. I know lying when I hear it."

"What about the vehicle?"

"Pickup truck. Maybe gold color."

Thomas tried another approach. "Kyle told us you'd asked the meat cutter where the meat came from, and he said Texas. Is this right?"

"Yeah, but he was lying. I could tell."

Exasperated, I asked, "Gee, Darren, does anyone tell you the truth?"

Thomas glared in my direction, and I just shook my head in disgust.

"A few more questions, and then we'll leave. Exactly why did you think the meat cutter was lying?"

"Shifty eyes."

Thomas closed his notebook and started to rise.

"And," Darren continued, "the first time I asked him, he said Nebraska. Then when I asked fifteen minutes later, he said Texas. The meat was already cut up, and the stamps were trimmed off with the fat. No way to verify where the carcasses came from."

Thomas sat back down. "Anything else?"

"Yeah. They had a hell of a lot of boxes of sausage casings. Way too many for that size business."

# 45

After seeing Darren's injuries, I tested my seatbelt to be assured the strap was tight.

"He could be a poster boy for wearing those," Thomas commented as we exited the hospital parking ramp.

"Well, he won't make a good trial witness, that's for sure. He's almost paranoid about being lied to."

"It happens," Thomas replied. "Cops get that way after a few years. However, we do save our impressions of the interview for later discussion. But," he paused, "you said what I was thinking."

"I couldn't help myself," I replied.

"What's your opinion about the sausage casings?" Thomas merged onto the northbound freeway.

"It seems possible. I suppose someone could stuff drugs into the casings just as easily as bulk sausage. It'd be easy to put a layer or two of the real sausage on top of the drugs. Then seal and label the boxes for shipping across town and beyond." I thought about it more. "Does this mean several of Javier's customers are drug dealers?"

"We're looking at his customers."

I pulled the ringing cell phone from my purse. "How are you doing, Jake?" I turned on the speaker so Thomas could hear.

"Good enough to get out of here. Except I don't know where my car is. Did Thomas have it towed?"

"No, Jake," Thomas answered. "It's still parked on the street where you left it. The ambulance took you before we knew it was your vehicle, and we decided to save you the impound lot fee and leave it there. You still have your keys, right?"

"Yeah, I have 'em. You two out on the town?"

"We're on our way back from Rochester," I reminded him. "Darren's in a lot worse shape than you are."

"Yeah. Well, thanks for the info. Drive careful," he advised and hung up.

"Jake doesn't like you," I interpreted for Thomas.

"I picked up on that earlier." He nodded, keeping an eye on the taillights ahead of us. "Why is that?"

"He says he's afraid I'll get into a dangerous situation with you."

"Does he know about your ex?"

"Absolutely not. No one else knows. And it better stay that way," I warned, raising my voice.

"It will. I gave you my word."

I turned to stare out the side window into the dark landscape.

Thomas pulled into a rest stop to make a call, hitting the speaker button while the phone rang.

"Who are the listed owners of the Mercado y Carne store near Cannon Falls, the place we talked about a few days ago? Any drug contacts? Have they all been checked out?" he asked.

"Three owners listed on the license application: Martino Torres, Louis Amando, and Robert Lopez."

"What about Sir Pedro's?" I asked. "Who's listed on their application?"

We heard paper shuffling until the agent found the document. "Logan Perez, Luis Perez, Tomás and Juanita Aguilar."

"Any chance Louis Amando could be Luis Perez-Amando or Luis Amando-Perez? Usually newer immigrants retain the family naming convention and use both the paternal and maternal surnames. How fully were their backgrounds checked?"

Again we heard paper shuffling. "They paid cash for the Cannon Falls location. Background checks didn't go any further by either the county or the Department of Agriculture."

"How much did they pay?" Thomas asked.

"Almost four hundred and thirty thousand."

"How did three recent immigrants scrape up that much money to buy the building outright? Who's backing them?"

"We're following the money. Spent hours diving into the background of these three, with nothing yet. Tax returns reveal modest income. Two of them live in rental properties; Aguliar owns a small farm near Rochester, runs a few head of cattle, and does vegetable gardening for farmers' markets in the area. The garden operation actually belongs to his brother."

"Nothing suspicious at all?" Thomas continued to prod.

"Yeah, a couple of things. For one, Amando's wife flies

to either Mexico or Panama every three months for about a week. She's never been caught with contraband, but the trip destinations are worth a closer look. We're on it, Thomas. We'll get back to you as soon as we pick up any more information." He disconnected.

"Do we just wait for them to call back?" I was irritated. "Surely they know all about the last names of Spanish speakers. How could they not have dug into it with a little more gusto? Javier is dead, the manager at Sir Pedro's is dead, and the guy who delivered stolen chemicals to both Javier's and Sir Pedro's is missing and possibly dead. Doesn't any of this raise a red flag?"

"How about we stop for a quick bite? You brought up a point I want to discuss some more," Thomas answered.

We slid into a booth at a truck stop, looked at the menus, and ordered our food before I asked, "What great point did I bring up?"

"Michael Lundeen. Sir Pedro's. Javier's. Like I said before, I don't like coincidences. You saw Michael on the security video at the meat market. We know he made after-hours deliveries to Javier and likely to Pedro's."

"If Lundeen was involved in drugs, I don't think he'd be working an eight-to-five job, even though he was incompetent."

"He would if he used and traded cleaning products for personal drugs," Thomas argued. "Maybe that's why things fell apart at Baker's Best."

"How did he get hired in the first place?" I asked as the waitress placed a bowl of wild rice soup in front of me. "Did someone recommend him? Who approved him? Let's say he used and sold a little. Wouldn't he make more money selling than his salary at Baker's Best? I don't see it, Thomas."

"It would explain why he's missing," he reasoned.

⁓

Jake couldn't remember the exact address of Michael Lundeen's house and directed the Uber driver to go slowly up and down several streets before they spotted his Jeep. When he brushed snow off the windshield, he was upset to find a ticket for parking without a neighborhood permit. One more insult in a lousy two days.

His first stop was the Craft Corner for a burger with fried onions and a pint of their winter ale. After the soggy vended sandwich in the factory yesterday, followed by tasteless hospital food, he was sure this would be pure heaven.

"What did ya do to your head?" the waitress asked after taking his order.

"Fell on concrete," Jake lied, not wanting to explain how stupid he'd been, walking into an ambush. He figured he was lucky Franklin didn't suspend him for leaving the factory to confront Lundeen.

What Jake had been trying to figure out, however, was why Lundeen had bashed his head with a shovel and left him to die on the garage floor. No reasonable answer came to mind. But his brain was groggy, and the stitches under the large bandage throbbed.

Still, questions persisted. Had Sheila called ahead and warned Lundeen? Maybe the lab tech was involved. He was definitely complicit in the missing reports.

He needed a talk with Sheila.

# 46

I spent the next morning reviewing the inspection reports of all the meat markets and the restaurants in my district that may have purchased product from Javier. I was familiar with one market that Jake and I had observed on Friday night.

A new owner had taken over this location eight months ago. At the time, we'd met briefly and did a walk-through to assess the equipment and the basic infrastructure. The owner didn't have great English skills, but we managed our communication, and I was satisfied with everything.

I hadn't inspected there since, but the address was due for a visit in the next thirty days. I put it on my schedule for today. Then I called Jake. "Can you find a half hour to inspect a small meat market with me today?"

"You going back to Javier's?"

"No. It's still closed. Remember the place Friday night where we saw the truck driver remove the large bags from the side door? On Twenty-eighth Street, the place before the baseball bat?"

"Is it on your inspection schedule?"

"Yes, and it's due. Today," I said, stretching the truth.

"What did Franklin say?"

"He's out of town for a conference. He told me to take another person along when I did these inspections." It seemed like a logical explanation.

"We're not supposed to do any more investigating, remember?"

"And your point is? Aren't you at all curious about the delivery we saw Friday night?"

"I'll meet you there at noon. We can do it over my lunch. I want to talk to you about Sheila anyway."

Jake was sitting in his car in the parking lot behind El Vaquero, music thumping from his radio, when I parked next to him. I was tempted to warn him about hearing loss but decided to let it go. There would be another opportunity.

We left our winter jackets in our vehicles and hustled to the front door. "What's the plan?" he asked.

"How about I keep him occupied in the first three minutes while you slip into the back before the employees get the signal we're here?"

"Works for me," Jake agreed as we entered.

El Vaquero was a typical medium-sized Latino market selling canned and packaged goods imported from Mexico and Central America. It had a small fresh-produce area on one side of the store and a long fresh-meat, poultry, and fish counter across the back. I recognized the owner working at a cash register. His blank look told me we had a thirty-second advantage before he could alert his employees.

"Hello, Robert, I'm Laura Neilson, and this is Jake Schaffner from the Health Department. It's time for your food safety inspection." We both showed our ID badge, and Jake headed to the meat counter.

"Ah, I see," Robert replied with a tight smile, staring at Jake's large bandage. "I am busy now. Can you come back later?" He looked down to continue counting money.

"We'll stay out of the way as much as possible," I promised. "Do you want to walk along with me, or would you rather just get the results before I leave?"

Robert turned his head to follow Jake. Then he looked at me. And back to see Jake disappearing behind the meat cases. "Maybe I go with him," he answered, pointing to Jake.

"Sure, if that's where you want to start, let's go." Since the Mexican telegraph had quickly sent news of Darren's raids, I assumed Robert was smart enough to have removed any uninspected meat or poultry—or drugs—before now. But such speculation presumed he was guilty before I started the inspection. I wanted to be fair and impartial until proven otherwise.

To give Jake extra time for a quick assessment and to talk with the employees, I dawdled along a canned goods aisle, checking the seals and inspecting labels for compliance.

"Your staff does a good job of looking at all of your imported foods," I commented, checking more items, killing time.

"*Sí*," he answered, still maintaining the tight, not-so-happy smile.

"How many employees do you have now?"

"*Um, cuarenta y cinco*, er, ah, forty-five," he replied, glancing again toward the meat counter.

"Looks like business is doing well," I dragged on.

Robert decided he'd had enough stalling and walked toward the back of the market.

We discovered Jake speaking in fractured Spanish with an employee who was packaging meat. Both were laughing, I figured about Jake mauling the language. Robert interrupted their repartee and spoke to his employee, who shook his head right to left to right. Nada. No more conversation with Jake.

With Robert at my elbow, I started a detailed evaluation of temperatures, cleanliness, sanitation practices, and all the other points on the inspection sheet. Each time I made a notation, he asked what it said.

The meat cooler stored only boxes of precut USDA-inspected meats and poultry but no sausage of any kind, which seemed unusual. The display counter didn't have any oxtail or flank steak for sale.

"Robert, your inventory is really low. No chorizo or flank?"

"Busy week," he replied.

"Do you make your own sausage here, or do you purchase it?"

"Make it here," he affirmed, turning his head to locate Jake.

"Did you ever get sausage from Javier?" I asked casually.

"No. Javier cheated me. The boxes were underweight, but he charged me for a whole box."

I stopped inspecting and looked him in the eye. "Did he do this to other customers? Cheat them."

"Maybe. Lotsa people no like him. I no surprised he's dead."

He said it with such conviction I was almost sure he wasn't involved in either the uninspected meat or the drugs. Almost. There was still the after-hours visit last Friday night.

I looked in the mop sink room and saw the cases of Pilot Chemicals. Had Robert purchased stolen goods from Michael Lundeen? Maybe he wasn't so innocent after all.

I continued talking and entering comments on my computer to keep Robert occupied. Not all of the documentation would result in a violation, but it gave Jake more time to assess other areas of the market and to chat with a few more employees.

Jake was ready to leave when Robert and I came down the produce aisle. Pointing to his watch, he reminded me of the time. "Gotta get back to the office. Talk to you later."

I nodded in agreement. "Just about finished."

Robert asked, "Is he your partner?"

"I guess you could say so. We pair up from time to time to verify each other's work."

"Who beat him up?"

"He fell on the ice."

"He no have a computer like you have," Robert noted. "Why not?"

"He's an observer this time. Next time, I'll do the same for him." My tongue burned from the mistruths.

The two of us assessed the fresh fruits and vegetables before I asked Robert to sign the inspection form on the computer screen. "If your email is correct on the line where you sign, I'll send you the report later this afternoon."

# 47

Before leaving, I walked across the poorly plowed parking lot to do a cursory inspection of the garbage enclosure. The dumpster lids were closed. I lifted the heavy plastic lid for a peek inside the dumpster and saw a large number of empty meat boxes streaked with frozen blood. Maybe they did have a busy week.

Instead of doing another inspection, I decided to go back to the office and compare notes with Jake before we were both too busy for accurate recall. But I didn't get beyond the Caribou Coffee at the next intersection. A tall skinny mocha, no whip, and an oatmeal cookie would satisfy my noisy stomach. It *was* made with skim milk, after all. And oatmeal *is* a whole grain.

I carried my guilty pleasures to a small corner table, hung my jacket on the chair, and removed the computer from its case to review the market inspection. Had I missed something? Something not quite right? What about the source of the chemicals? Why didn't I ask him about the Friday night delivery?

I called Jake. "Would you do me a favor and call Pilot Chemicals to verify Robert is a customer?"

"Hi to you too. Yeah, I'll make the inquiry this afternoon," Jake confirmed. "I've got a whale of a headache and am off the computer for a while."

"Did you get any information from the meat counter employee?" I asked before devouring a chunk of cookie.

"He said they just started getting boxed cut meat last week. They'd been receiving whole beef and pork carcasses, but their supplier went out of business. Then you walked in, and he clammed up. Did you see all the empty boxes in the dumpster?"

"Yes, I saw them. It sounds like Robert continued using Javier longer than he admitted."

"They would have heard about Darren's raids," Jake added. "But if those were uninspected carcasses being removed Friday night, Robert sure took a risk waiting that long."

"Where would he have hidden such bulky stuff?" I wondered.

"His home garage, maybe in the dumpster. In this cold, either would work. There'd be no spoilage or odor."

"But who picked them up Friday night?"

"That's easy. The guy with the baseball bat."

"And did you learn anything from the cute little woman at the cash register?"

"Only that her English is worse than my Spanish." Jake laughed.

Before leaving the coffee shop, I left a message for Thomas. "Did anybody follow up on the addresses Jake and I gave the police for the stores where the white delivery truck stopped? In particular, I'm interested in El Vaquero Market. Call me when you have time." Then I drove back to see Robert.

Thomas texted back: "Will check it out. Are you there now? Alone?"

Both he and Franklin were beginning to annoy me. I ignored the message.

Robert was in his small one-desk, one-chair office completing a phone order when I entered. He looked at me, nodded, and finished his requests. I stood in front of the closed door, arms crossed.

"Did you forget something?" Robert asked after he hung up the phone.

"Friday night."

Furling his brows, Robert cocked his head. "Friday night?"

"Come on, Robert. The van driver who loaded large bags about the shape of carcasses onto his truck. After nine p.m." I continued in short, clipped words. "Tell me the truth."

Robert took a deep breath, folded his hands on the desk, and stared at me. He swallowed several times, never breaking eye contact. "*Senorita, yo no—*"

"English, Robert," I demanded. "Explain in English."

"Will I go to jail?" he whispered. "Or be deported?"

"It's likely the only thing you'll get is a fine."

His body sagged with relief, leaning back in the chair. "Javier could send meat much cheaper than my other suppliers. I did not ask questions. When Javier was murdered, another hombre stopped and said he give me the same deal. I say, 'Why not?'"

Running his fingers over his scalp, Robert exhaled a turbulence of fear. "But then we hear about Department of Agriculture looking for bad meat with no stamp. I look at my meat. It's no good. So I call the man, and he says he pick it up Friday. I ask what I do with it until then. He say it's my problem. So I hide it all in my truck for two days."

"Can you remember if the meat from Javier had an inspection stamp?" I asked.

"Maybe. Maybe not. We not look very close. Sometimes meat not a good color, but we use many spices, and it look okay. Customers not bring it back." Fear-tainted sweat beaded on his forehead.

I pressed for more information. "Robert, who picked up the meat Friday night?"

"Don't know." He shrugged. "We just get a call that tell me they coming to pick it up."

"You didn't recognize him?"

"No." He shook his head vigorously. "No." Robert dropped his head into waiting hands. "What will happen now?"

"I didn't find anything illegal here today, and I've always considered you a good store owner. But if you're involved with drug transportation, it's another ball game."

*Damn, I just used a sports analogy. Franklin would be so proud.*

"No, no. No drugs. It is too dangerous to get involved with drugs," Robert affirmed, sinking into his chair.

"I'll take your word, but if anything at all connected with uninspected meat or drugs comes up again, my support will be gone."

"*Sí,*" he replied, exhaling deep relief.

"Help me find the supplier, Robert. Do you have the invoices from the last company after Javier?"

"Only cash," Robert replied, shaking his head. "Javier only wanted cash. Same with the other one."

"But you must have the telephone number for the new supplier," I insisted. "Can you find it?"

Robert opened his desk drawer to search for the information.

We were interrupted by a firm knocking on the office door. "Laura, are you in there?" Thomas shouted, "Police. Open up!"

"What are you doing here?" I asked, jerking the door open. "What's happened?"

Robert's face was ashen, eyes wide, exposing deep fear. "Police?" he whispered, looking at me, his hand still in the drawer.

Thomas pointed his weapon and ordered, "Hands on the desk." Robert complied.

"Put your gun away," I yelled. "What are you doing here?"

Thomas looked at me, turned to scrutinize Robert, and then back to me. "I thought you were in trouble."

"Oh, Thomas," I said, shaking my head. "We'll talk about this later."

As Robert collapsed into a sinkhole of fear, I turned to him. "This is my friend Thomas Garcia. Thomas, this is Robert, owner of this market. He has been telling me a very interesting story."

Thomas spoke in Spanish, easing tension in the tiny, airless office. Robert responded warily, but then something

Thomas said broke the barrier, and the manager's words rushed out in an unchecked flow.

I recognized Javier's name a couple times but otherwise couldn't follow the conversation. Thomas kept nodding, and Robert kept talking. Five minutes later, they both stopped and looked at me.

"What?" I replied.

"He'll help us, and he'll help you," Thomas assured me, relaying their conversation. Indeed, Robert had been asked if he wanted to be a drug pickup location, but he refused, citing cops as his customers for his excuse. Javier had mocked him for his cowardice and then started sending boxes of underweight products and charging him more for cutting the meat. At that point, Robert ordered only the whole carcass and hired a butcher/sausage maker.

"How long ago was this?" I asked.

Robert answered, "One month ago. But I think Javier was dealing drugs a long time. He had lots of money this year."

"And you have the phone number for the new seller, correct?" I asked.

"*Sí,*" he answered, pulled his cell phone from the drawer, and held it for us to read.

After noting the cell number, Thomas turned to leave. "I'll leave you two to your work."

"Wait. You don't want to pursue this?"

"The meat investigation belongs to Ag. I'll check the phone number and give it to the drug guys, but I'll bet it's from a disposable phone, and it can't be traced. See you tonight?" he asked before opening the door to leave.

"Call me later," I replied, waving him out.

He winked and left.

"He likes you." Robert smiled for the first time in an hour.

Ignoring his comment, I stuck to business. "Robert, you will still be in big trouble if Ag asks to see back receipts and invoices for your meat. You do have them for the product in your store right now, correct?"

"Yes, yes. No problem." He turned his chair to the file cabinet and retrieved a folder.

I reviewed his paperwork and advised, "Even if you pay cash, always, always get a receipt from now on."

# 48

I called Jake as soon as I returned to the office. "Do you still have the list of addresses where the white truck stopped Friday night?"

"Of course. Give me a sec to find it." I heard papers rustling and mild cursing. "It's not here, so it must be in the car. Why do you want it?"

"Because the driver definitely was picking up uninspected meat from El Vaquero. I just talked to Robert, and he confirmed it. He was desperate to get rid of it. So if that's the case, then what was delivered to the other places? The same old meat?"

"Didn't the cops follow up?"

"Doesn't appear so. As Thomas said, it's Ag's domain." I was frustrated about his declaration, even though he was right.

"Since Darren is out of commission for a while, maybe it is your domain after all," Jake suggested.

"First of all, the other address actually in my district is not due for an inspection for nine months. Ergo, I have no good reason to go there. And you recall what Franklin said, correct?"

Jake mumbled, "Uh-huh."

"On another topic, what did you find out from Pilot Chemicals? Is Robert paying for his supply?"

"Yeah, he is. The clerk I talked to said Robert orders supplies on a regular basis. This keeps Michael Lundeen out of Robert's place."

"Good. I like Robert." I turned on the computer to upload Robert's inspection.

"Why don't you do an off-the-record inspection at the other place? What's the address? I could go along this afternoon after four," Jake pressed.

"What's your interest?"

"I wanna find out who was swinging the baseball bat at my car."

⸎

At precisely 4 p.m., Jake entered my cubicle wearing his parka and gloves. "Ready to go?"

"It's obvious you are. Just don't forget this place actually doesn't require an inspection until next spring."

"Yeah, but it needs one now," Jake asserted. "I'm following up on a foodborne illness complaint."

"Which complaint is this?" I asked suspiciously.

"This one," he announced as he laid the form on my desk.

"Came in an hour ago, huh? Pretty convenient, isn't it?"

"Yes, it is," he replied with a wry smile. "In fact, it's so recent, I'll bet the info hasn't even been logged into the database yet."

"Now who's crazy? You better hope Franklin doesn't learn anything about this escapade, or I'll be helping you scrub the floors in the lab for the next month."

"No worries," he assured me.

Instead of checking out a state car, Jake drove his Jeep. Ostensibly it would be faster to drive straight home from the market versus returning the state vehicle. It also eliminated any official link to our visit. But since my car was parked in the ramp, the return was still required.

"How are you planning to approach this?" I asked as he merged onto the freeway.

"We can keep it short and sweet. I'll flash the complaint form and tell them I'm working with State Ag and want to look at their purchasing invoices to determine where they buy their meat because there's some *E. coli* around. Why don't you walk in a minute ahead of me and browse the aisles and meat case? Keep an eye open for who does what when I talk to the manager."

"Don't get out of my sight," I demanded. "Not even for one second."

He nodded in agreement.

As we approached the address, I began to feel uneasy. Impending darkness cast icy shadows on unshoveled sidewalks, and unlit windows offered no beacons of warmth. An aging frame house on the corner was boarded up, the condemnation sign recognizable by its neon orange glow as it flapped in the wind. Jake dropped me off in a snow bank a block away, and I walked briskly toward the market, passing the liquor store and the fast cash loan outlet without glancing into either.

Joe's Fourth Street Market was smaller than most of those I inspected, only five short aisles of dry foods and one of produce. I grabbed a small plastic grocery basket and wandered toward the produce section, checking cans for dents, bulges, and proper labels along the way. The inventory was sparse and made me wonder how they made a profit.

When Jake entered, I was staring at the bagged celery, wilted green peppers, and wrapped heads of browning iceberg lettuce. I moved closer to the meat cases, where I could watch the employees and maybe hear most of what Jake was saying.

He approached the lone female checkout employee, flashed his ID badge, and explained he was looking for contaminated beef that had caused an illness. He said the sick person had told the Health Department some of the meat was purchased from this location. He wanted to speak to the owner or manager.

She looked at Jake's complaint form, turned away, and disappeared behind a nearby door.

Jake waited. I continued to watch the meat prep area. Would the owner go there first before hearing about the complaint?

A minute later, a short, burly man with a full beard appeared with the cashier from behind the door to see Jake. She walked to the back of the store and motioned two employees toward the storage area.

I moved to a spot behind the bread display case, where I could see her arms punctuating her words and their heads nodding in agreement before all three sidled into the unlit back corner.

When I turned back to look for Jake, he was gone. And so was the owner. Where did they go? A customer rolled her cart to the checkout. Two more people walked in the front door. The first cashier had not returned, and another young man began scanning the items from the grocery cart. I looked at my watch. Two minutes? Three? Where was he?

"Can I help you?" the first cashier asked me on her return from the back room.

"Yes, you can," I said, glaring at her. "I want to see the owner. Right. Now." I produced my ID badge.

Her eyes broadcast the lie. "He's not here."

"Yes, he is here," I countered. "He was talking to the gentleman from the Health Department less than three minutes ago. I want to see him. Now."

She glared back and turned to walk away. I grabbed her arm and held on. "Either now, or I'll call the police." There was no way she was leaving.

She twisted with a painful grimace and pulled her arm out of my grasp. "This way."

I followed her to the door behind the checkout lane. She opened it and pointed to the basement. "Down there."

My immediate fear was finding Jake lying in a lifeless mass at the bottom. Was he pushed down the old wooden steps? Would she push me?

"Stand over there so I can watch you," I ordered.

On the top step, grasping the stair railing with one hand and watching her the entire time, I yelled, "Jake, are you down there?"

Nothing.

"Jake," I called louder. "Can you hear me?"

One. Two. Three. Four. Five seconds passed.

"I'm calling the police," I shouted in her face.

Noise from the basement. A door opened. Footsteps.

"It's okay, Laura. I'm fine," Jake assured me on his way up.

I sagged against the wall. The cashier bolted downstairs, leaving Jake and me behind the checkout counter facing the angry frowns of several shoppers.

"Where were you?" I hissed. "You were supposed to stay in my sight."

"I thought you saw us. We went to his office to find the meat invoices."

"And did you?"

"Of course not," he replied as he urged me toward the front door. "A litany of excuses. He now claims the papers may be in the meat-cutting room. We need to get out of here."

"But what about them?" I asked, turning to see where the cashier had gone.

"Call Thomas. This guy pretty much admitted receiving drugs."

"Pretty much admitted? What does that mean?" I asked as we hustled along the deserted sidewalk.

"It means last Friday he took an after-hours delivery for someone else to pick up Saturday. And he was making a panicky phone call when I left."

We waited in Jake's car until we heard sirens. Marked and unmarked cars pulled in front of the market and blocked the alley behind it. Four uniforms and two undercover cops barged through the front door with weapons drawn.

"This is enough excitement for the day," I announced as

we drove away from the curb into early November darkness. "And don't forget my car is in the ramp."

"Yeah, I remember." He turned east onto 31st Street. While waiting at a red light, he asked, "What do you think about our Sheila at the factory? Is she telling us the truth about everything, or is she tighter with Michael Lundeen than we realize?"

"What makes you ask that?"

"It was too convenient that Lundeen didn't answer his front door. I think Sheila tipped him off, and he was waiting for me in the garage." He flipped a turn signal and tried to ease into the left lane.

"How would Lundeen have known you'd even look in the garage, Jake?"

"If it wasn't him, then who was it? And where is he now? I'm betting Sheila knows."

"I don't think so. She was just way too pleased to have us in the factory. Why don't we just call and ask her? It's not quite five; she's still in the office."

My call went to voicemail. "Sheila, it's Laura from the Health Department. We're hoping you can help us find Michael Lundeen. Do you know how to contact him?"

# 49

By the time I returned home, my mind was tangled in a rat's maze of questions and possibilities with no clear path to answers.

Bringing Michael Lundeen to trial for his neglect and the death of at least two people who consumed the potpies would take months and months. Under the Park Doctrine, the Department of Justice would likely pursue him and the company president for criminal charges, but by then the piece of scum might have completely disappeared.

As soon as I opened the door, Dude wound himself around my leg and meowed pitifully. I grabbed the closest can of Fancy Feast, opened it, and dumped a portion into a clean bowl before removing my coat.

"Here. No complaints, okay? I have things to do."

I fixed a quick omelet and tossed a salad. Between bites, I drew up a list of questions that still hadn't been answered.

My first phone call went to voicemail. "Thomas, who is the real Michael Lundeen? If the one we know from Baker's Best is actually Michael Russell, where's the other one?"

Call number two went to Sheila. Voicemail again. "Can

you find the application and résumé for Michael Lundeen and text or scan a copy to me? Who were his references? Who interviewed him? Please contact me asap."

I scraped some egg pieces into the grateful cat's dish, poured a glass of red zin, grabbed the notes, sank into my wing chair, and began listing more questions while waiting for the phone to ring.

It didn't take long.

"The real Michael Lundeen," Thomas announced without even saying hello, "died eighteen months ago and is buried in Des Moines, Iowa. According to his obit, he was fifty-two years old and was a supervisor for Belmont Foods. No suspicious cause of death."

"Ah," I speculated, "this gave the fake Michael credentials for the Baker's Best job. What I still can't understand is how he made it through an interview, unless our phony guy had basic experience from a food production facility."

"Michael Russell is a con man, Laura. He could sell a beach umbrella to an Eskimo."

"So where is he now?"

"We're trying to track him, but either he has a lot of cash, or he's already assumed a new identity. No credit or debit cards in either name have been used, nothing on our radar at all," Thomas conceded.

"Jake thinks Sheila knows where he is, but I'm not so sure. Has your investigation included her?"

"Nothing has come up pointing to her."

"Good. I like her."

"Speaking of like, how about dinner Tuesday night?"

"Ah, what an interesting segue, Detective."

"Yeah, I'm really good at that." He laughed. "Maybe you can define that word for me over a plate of pasta. Pick you up at six?"

"It works," I answered with a smile I was sure he could hear.

Sheila's call came a half hour later.

"Laura, I left the office early. To answer your first question, no, I don't know how to contact Michael. And right now we're still waiting for approval from the feds to reopen. They inspected the Ohio factory and weren't happy with that operation either. There's a reorganization going on at headquarters, plus they need to hire a manager and additional staff for this location. It's going to take a while."

Dude jumped on my lap, landing on the pad of paper and flipping the pencil onto the floor. He rested his paws on my chest and rubbed his purring head under my chin. I pulled the pad out and placed it on the side table, where I could read my questions for Sheila. In the commotion, the cell nearly slipped out of my hand.

"Hold on a sec, Sheila. I'm going to put you on speaker so I can deal with this pesky cat and retrieve my pencil."

"I thought I heard purring. So," she continued before I could remove the cat or search for the pencil, "Michael Lundeen was hired without an interview. The previous manager retired for health reasons, but he was consulted about the applications for his replacement. He actually recommended Michael. Said they'd met at a conference, and he knew Michael would do a great job. End of process."

"No orientation into your system? He just shows up and starts working?"

"Almost like that," Sheila confirmed. "Someone from Ohio flew up and talked to Michael for an hour, signed the hiring papers, and flew back the same day. Bingo, we've got a new factory manager. I have the paperwork. You want to see it?"

"You have his résumé?" I asked.

"Sure. I made copies of everything the cops wanted. They didn't tell me not to share. How soon do you want the info?"

"Tomorrow? I'd also like to get back into his office."

"Not a problem," Sheila assured me. "Stop by later in the afternoon."

"Is after five too late?"

"That's fine. See you then, Laura."

I remembered opening one cardboard box in Michael's office that appeared to be personal items, including an obituary. At the time, I put it aside, but now I wondered if there was a clue in the box that might find a trail to the imposter.

Tomorrow's plan also included getting copies of Javier's Market records from Ag. The investigation of uninspected meat had withered since Darren's car accident, and it was unlikely any further action would be taken soon. I still hoped those records might reveal a lead or two.

# 50

"Did you hear from Sheila?" Jake asked, setting his can of cola on the desk next to my empty cup and sitting down.

"Coffee not made yet?" I nodded at the cup.

"Nah. Too early," he answered, totally missing the point.

"Yes, I did hear from Sheila," I continued, "and she'll stay later at the office until we get there this afternoon. She has the phony Michael Lundeen's personnel file, and I want another look at those boxes in his office."

"Didn't the cops take his file? I assumed they would be hot on his tail after the guy bashed my head open." Jake touched the bandage and winced.

"She made copies first. Your head hurt?"

"Yeah, worse today. Doc says I should cut my hours to half time for a few weeks and limit computer work. Like that's possible."

"Did you talk to Franklin?" I asked, rolling back in my chair to look him directly in the eyes.

"Not yet." He stared at the floor, avoiding me.

"Maybe you shouldn't drive out there this afternoon."

"No chance of that. But I *am* going to look behind doors before entering," Jake said over his shoulder as he left.

The pool secretary at Ag wasn't sure who could take my phone call. She insisted Darren was out of the office and didn't seem to understand that anyone on his team would be fine. She didn't have a team list, just a list of names and phone numbers.

"Fine. Ring Darren's phone, and I'll just wait until someone finally answers."

"But he's not here, so why would I put you through to his line?"

"Because I expect someone in meat inspections will eventually answer it," I replied in my best Minnesota-nice patience.

"Oh, meat inspections. Why didn't you say so?" the ditz replied. "Here you go."

Darren's coworker agreed to lend out Javier's documents, affirming he wanted them returned. He was planning to be near my office later this morning and would drop off the packet. An hour later, it was on my desk.

I called Jake. "Are you resting your eyes?"

"What's up?"

"I have all Javier's files from Ag. Have time to help me sort through them one last time?"

"Everybody has already scrutinized those docs. What do you think you can find that they haven't?"

"I'm not sure. I just know something has been overlooked. Javier's office was trashed and so was his house, so I'm betting whoever killed him never found what he wanted. But if you're not feeling well, it's fine."

"I'll be there in a half hour. I'll need a computer break by then."

An hour later, Jake's outstretched hand entered my cubicle holding a cappuccino.

"I come with a peace offering," he announced with a sheepish smile, setting it on my desk. "I'm late, and I apologize for carping at you. My patience is wearing thin this week." He sank into a chair. "What am I looking for?"

"I'm not exactly sure. Thomas said we'd know when we found it," I responded between sips of the hot beverage.

"Yeah, well, let's hope he's right," Jake said, popping a can of cola. "I have forty-five minutes before Franklin starts looking for me."

"What did you do now?"

"It's what I haven't done. Still getting more complaints from potpie eaters. Have to take more breaks due to headaches."

"You sure you want to do this?"

"Yeah, it's a different kind of break. I'll be fine." He closed his eyes for a few seconds before picking up a stack of papers.

We started with invoices, looking not only for wholesale meat deliveries but also for chemicals. A lack of invoices for cleaning products would give us an idea of the approximate time when Javier started purchasing from Michael Lundeen. We also hoped to determine when the large shipments of sausage casings began since it seemed this date would indicate when the drug distribution had started.

We looked at scribbled notes on the backs of orders and invoices. We were surprised to find three inspection reports and pulled those for later scrutiny.

Jake caved first. "Thomas is wrong. There's nothing I found in this mess that gives any more info than we already know. I've got to get back to my desk."

"I agree. Thanks for the help. See you at four-thirty for a last look at the factory."

# 51

Jake wasn't the only one behind on work. I skipped lunch and did three inspections in the afternoon. I asked each manager who signed my computer form how long they kept the inspection reports. Two said a week or two, until they'd checked off all the corrections. One manager confirmed he kept old reports for three months. Which made me wonder about the old reports in Javier's files.

I met Jake in the parking ramp after four-thirty and hopped into his warm vehicle. The daylight was already snuffed out by the heavy clouds of November when he merged onto the freeway. We became just another snag in the rush-hour snarl, knotting and loosening all the way to the southwestern sub-urbs. I called Sheila to let her know we were close but would be late due to traffic.

"I'll be here. The accounting staff is working overtime pulling together all the numbers they want in Ohio. I'm the gopher until they finish."

Jake had Jazz88 on the radio, bopping his hand on the

steering wheel between traffic reports. "Who do you think will get the ax in Ohio?" he asked.

"Surely whoever hired Lundeen. I'd guess also the VP and probably the human resources director. If what Sheila says is correct and the other factory also has problems, the president will be gone as well."

"If the Department of Justice gets involved, they may see some jail time. Warms my heart," Jake said, still tapping to the music.

I texted Sheila as we pulled into the factory parking lot, and she met us at the delivery door.

"You'd be interested to know," she said with obvious excitement as we walked down the dark unheated hallway, "that Michael called about a half hour ago and said he was coming to pick up his personal items. Said he knew he was fired and just wanted to clear out his stuff."

"He's still around?" I was stunned.

"I told him we'd already thrown it all out and good riddance."

"You actually said that?" Jake said, laughing.

"Of course I did. He spewed a litany of curses and threatened to shoot me on sight."

"You're not worried?" I asked.

"Nah, he talked like that all the time. Just a big jerk."

She unlocked the office door and switched on the overhead lights. "His crap is in those boxes, and a copy of his personnel file was accidently left on the table. Have fun."

"If Michael wants his boxes, there has to be something

important in them he doesn't want found," I surmised, removing my coat and gloves.

Jake nodded, hung his jacket on a chair, and opened the cardboard flaps. I grabbed the personnel file.

A messaging notice on my phone pinged simultaneously with Jake's. It came from Thomas: "Lundeen still in cities. Stay alert."

"What the hell does that mean?" Jake exclaimed. "Is the guy trailing us with an AK47?"

"Be real," I said. "He steals chemicals, not weapons." I lifted a brown paper box and set it on the table. "Let's take a closer look."

It didn't take long for our first discovery. "Look at this," Jake said. "Obit for the real Michael Lundeen. He died about eighteen months ago."

"That's not the one I saw before. If I recall correctly, it was for someone with the surname of Russell. See if you can find anything with that name."

Digging through a second box, I came upon a disposable cell phone. "Aha, look what we have here. Maybe this is what he wanted." I held the "on" button down. "Dead battery."

"Maybe not," Jake said. "Let's see if Sheila has a charging cord." He took the silent phone and left in search of a lifeline.

I was reading the obit for James Russell when Jake returned with the prize.

"Ta-da," he announced as he plugged one end of the cord into the wall and the other into the cell phone. "Sheila to the rescue."

I held up the yellowed newspaper item. "This is the obit I

found before. I think maybe he was our phony Michael's family member. By the age of the person, I'd guess he might have been Michael's father. Why else would he have this?" I kept reading. "It says James Russell has three sons: John, Wayne, and Arthur. Maybe one of them assumed a new name."

Setting it aside, I kept sifting through the contents.

*Blaaat.* The abrupt noise crashed through the silence of the factory. *Blaaat.* It rumbled again. "What the hell?" Jake bolted upright.

"Receiving dock door. Someone wants in pretty badly." *Is it Lundeen, coming to look for his boxes despite Sheila's assertion she had trashed them?*

I pushed my chair back and heard it slam on the floor. *Blaaat.* Again the bell rang. I ran out the door and almost collided with Sheila exiting her office.

"Do you have security cameras on the dock?" I asked as we sprinted toward the sound. "He doesn't have a master key, does he?"

"Locks were all changed yesterday, so if it's Michael, he won't get in," she confirmed, racing down the steps to the factory floor.

"You're not going to open the door to see who it is, are you?" The warning from Thomas repeated itself over and over. *Stay alert, stay alert.*

"Hell, no," she exclaimed. "The security camera monitor is in the supervisor's office."

By the time she found the light switch and turned on the screen, the insistent ringing had ceased, and all we saw was an empty dock.

"Any more cameras for the parking lot?" I asked. "Are there backup tapes?"

"No to both. Whoever it was is gone anyway." She hit the off button. "Could have been a vendor we forgot to notify."

"At six p.m.? I don't think so, Sheila."

"Well, he's gone," she answered with more confidence than I had.

"Who was it?" Jake asked when I returned.

"Don't know, but what if it was Lundeen? There must be something here he really wants."

"This," Jake said, holding the partially charged cell in his hand. "Idiot didn't use a password. I'm guessing all these phone numbers will trace to somebody illegal. Why else use a disposable? Let's try a couple and see who answers," he continued, pressing his finger on the screen. We listened while it rang and rang with no message service.

"Was it a local number?"

"Yeah, a 612 area code. In Minneapolis somewhere. Here's another one in the city that shows up several times on his list."

Another dead end.

"Maybe all his contacts used disposables," I reasoned. "Does he have any email on it?"

"Nope. But he does have a camera. Let's see if he has anything there," Jake said, opening the app. "Aha, a few photos and a short video. They don't look like much. What do you think?" he asked and handed the phone to me.

The first five photos were taken after dark in what looked like an empty snowy parking lot. The sixth picture was a blurry image of someone walking from left to right. The next photo showed the same image walking in the other direction. Photo number eight showed a second person behind the first one. In the video, the two blurry images were standing face to face.

"You okay?" Jake asked. "You look like you've seen a ghost."

"I know what this is," I answered, pointing at the phone. "This is Javier's parking lot, and this photo right here," I held it for him to inspect, "shows Javier and his assailant just before he was killed. It means Michael was there. Either an accomplice or a witness."

Jake took the phone and inspected the grainy image. "How can you be sure it's Javier?"

"It's taken from the same angle as the security photos Thomas showed me. I'm positive."

"But it's impossible to see who these people are," Jake countered.

"I'm betting fine tuning could tame the blur enough to figure it out. I'm calling Thomas."

Voicemail answered, and I left a message describing the phone and the other information we'd discovered. "We'll take the phone with us," Jake said, setting it on his briefcase.

Thirty minutes later, Sheila opened the door and announced, "Okay, guys, I'm locking it up. You can take the boxes with you for all I care."

"We'll take this stuff," I answered, holding a small pile of papers. "And the phone. We think these boxes will all be subpoenaed, but we want to get this to Thomas tonight."

Jake handed her a handwritten document. "Please sign this saying we received these items. Each one is detailed on this list."

"Wow, you sure are precise," Sheila replied as she looked at the list. "This is all really necessary?"

"At this point, we don't want any glitches," I confirmed.

"Include the date and time, Sheila," Jake directed. "We'll both sign, and then you can make a copy for your records."

"You'd think this was a murder case instead of contaminated food," Sheila said as she handed the pen to Jake.

# 52

I was worried for Sheila and for us. "What if he's waiting in the parking lot for a chance to get inside? Or worse?"

"We'll check the lot before we leave," Jake assured me. "If there's another car out there, we'll wait."

"Wait for what?"

"You'll call Thomas to the rescue."

"So now he's okay?" *Damn, here we go again.*

Jake was peeved. "Yeah, now he's okay."

"Sorry," I mumbled, zipping my coat.

Sheila popped in the door and gave Jake copies of the signed document. Bundled in a gray down jacket, black wool scarf wound around her neck almost up to her nose, and black knee-high boots, she was ready to leave. "I'll go out with you," she announced and waited until we'd put our papers and the phone in Jake's briefcase and put on our jackets.

When we left through the dock door, I looked for a third set of footprints on the steps or approaching the dock but saw nothing except indistinguishable wind-blurred ridges. It didn't mean someone wasn't still lurking in the dark corners, but there were only two cars in the parking lot, Jake's and Sheila's.

We waited for Sheila to start her car, turn on the lights, and drive away.

Jake entered the side street and barely drove the speed limit. It wasn't his normal style.

"Why so slow?"

"Watching the rear to see if we're being followed. I don't trust the guy. Just because his car wasn't there doesn't mean he's not watching Sheila or us. I told her to call me as soon as she gets home and to lock up."

By the time he merged onto the freeway, we were sure no one was trailing us, leaving Jake relaxed as much as possible in heavy traffic.

"Get any more complaints from the widow with the crappy lawyer?" he asked, turning on the left turn signal before sliding into the center lane.

"Ah, Dorothy. I need to call her."

"Why? You don't have to follow up anymore. We have all the information."

"She needs other resources. She's been emotionally abused, possibly physically as well." I stared out the windshield, remembering.

"You can refer her to mental health services or a support group, can't you?"

"Last time we talked, she wouldn't even consider assistance. I'm worried about her."

"Not your problem, Laura. Let it go."

"She's in a bad place and needs help. I can't just drop it."

*Should I tell him?*

"Whatever," he answered, flipping the turn signal again.

Jake merged back into the right lane. "I'm taking surface streets. They have to be faster than this. Check your map app to find a reasonable alternative."

Google maps suggested a shorter route, albeit only by three minutes. Jake exited on West Lake Street and crept slowly from stoplight to stoplight. He turned off the radio. "Alright if we don't have any music? My headache's back."

"Do you want me to drive?"

"Nah, I can manage."

As we reached a familiar intersection in the Uptown neighborhood, Jake asked, "Why exactly do you care so much about that woman?"

I knew where this was going and also where I didn't want to go. Choosing my words with care, I replied, "You mean Dorothy. I'm concerned because I know women who have been abused, and they need a lot of support and counseling. She's of the generation where counseling implies a weakness and is something not discussed openly."

"But why can't you just refer her?" he repeated.

"Because I'm afraid she'll be lost in the system, primarily due to her age. That's strange." I grabbed a diversion as we passed Sir Pedro's. "Some dining room lights are on. They haven't been given permission to reopen."

"Maybe getting ready to?"

"No. There hasn't been an application for new owners."

"Moving equipment out under the cloak of darkness?" Jake suggested as he turned right at the corner and then right into an alley.

"Where are you going?"

"Back to Sir Pedro's. Let's find out what's happening."

"This is dumb, Jake. Talk about getting into dangerous situations."

"We'll just observe for a few minutes, that's all." He stopped in the alley next to the dumpsters, turning off the engine.

A gray SUV was parked near the back door.

"He can't put much equipment in that vehicle," I said. "Maybe it's just a prospective new owner surveying the property."

"Then where's the realtor's car?"

"You're making this into some kind of illegal activity when it probably isn't at all."

"*Probably*? Do I detect a hint of suspicion?" He opened his door and unsnapped his seatbelt.

"Where are you going?

"Gonna check it out."

My phone rang, interrupting my protest.

"Answer your call." He closed the door without a sound.

It was Thomas. "Where'd you find the cell phone?"

"In his personal boxes at the factory. He had two small moving boxes filled with photos and old newspaper clippings, including the obituary for the real Michael Lundeen and another one most likely for his father. We tried calling a few numbers on the phone, but they were disconnected."

"Don't suppose you considered wearing gloves while you did this?"

"Ugh. No. I'm sorry. It didn't cross my mind."

"But you do have chain-of-evidence documents for the phone and the other items you took, correct?"

"Yes, we know how to do that," I replied, relieved we didn't mess up everything.

"Where are you? I can meet you and pick it up."

"We can bring it to the police station as soon as we leave here," I said, watching Jake enter the back door.

"Where is *here*?"

"Sir Pedro's. There was a light on and a car parked in the back, so we stopped to take a look, and then Jake had the bright idea to check it out. He just went inside."

"What the hell is he thinking? Isn't one bashed temple enough for him?"

The silence hung like an executioner's axe.

"Stay inside the car," he ordered. "I'm on my way."

Before I could ask how long it would take, he ended the call. Two minutes passed. I checked my phone just to be sure Jake hadn't texted.

No Jake.

No Thomas either.

# 53

Jake slid in the back door and heard someone speaking forcefully in Spanish. From the pauses between loud outbursts, he guessed it was a phone conversation. While his rudimentary language skills were not good enough to understand any of it, he recognized anger when he heard it.

The kitchen was unlit, but a sliver of light coming from the open dining door was enough to detect the edge of a worktable and the wire storage racks along the wall. Jake moved cautiously forward, hoping to see the speaker.

Instead, the voice started moving closer to him. The nearest escape from detection turned out to be the mop closet. He closed the door behind him, leaving a narrow slit of dim light to illuminate hanging mops and brooms. One step at a time, he moved toward the back corner, knowing if he elbowed even one broom handle, the noise would broadcast his location.

He heard the back door open.

"'Bout time you got here," the angry voice barked in English.

"Yeah, well, I had a problem," the new voice growled.

The second guy sounded familiar. Jake closed his eyes to visualize a face, but nothing appeared.

"You got it or not, *amigo*?"

"I ain't your *amigo*, Pedro. I put it in a lock box. You give me the money, I give you the key and disappear."

"That no gonna work," Pedro said. "I need to see the pictures before you get paid."

Jake knew who owned the second voice. His muscles tightened with fury, and the stitches on his head throbbed for revenge. But when he saw the shadow of Michael Lundeen walk past, he stood as still as the mops.

"Look, I've got the cops looking for me because you hit that state inspector and he almost died in my garage," Michael argued. "If I got stopped, they'd find the phone, and you'd already be in jail. They have no proof without it, and I'm not saying nuthin' to no one. I just want out of here."

"No phone, no money," Pedro repeated.

Jake wanted to burst out from the dark closet to confront the guy who bashed his head but was certain it would cause him even more trouble. In the long run, smelling like a moldy mop was preferable to another gurney ride.

~

I saw headlights from a second car sweep the parking lot, instinctively sank to the car floor, and counted fifteen seconds before daring to peek out the window. The second vehicle parked next to the first one. The driver looked around and entered the back door.

My heart beat so loudly I was sure he'd heard it. Sliding back on the floor, I called Thomas again. No answer. He had to be close. Should I warn Jake? No, even a text message would make noise.

Someone tapped on the driver's side window. I froze. Maybe the guy in the car had seen me after all. *What have I gotten into?*

"Laura," a familiar voice called. "Open up."

Whew. I flipped the locks for Thomas to open the passenger door.

"Quick," he ordered. "Slip out, stay low, and get behind the car." Thomas pushed the door shut to kill the inside light.

"Any changes?" he asked as we crouched behind Jake's Jeep.

"A second person just arrived," I explained, shivering in the cold wind.

"We need to move to the alley for better cover. Then tell me what you saw."

We ran to his car parked behind two massive dumpsters, shielded from view of the restaurant. He continued the questions. "How many in the second car?"

"I saw only one."

"Jake?"

"Nothing," I answered, shaking my head.

Softly touching my cheek, he offered words of reassurance. "He'll be fine." I don't think either of us believed it.

Another set of headlights drove into the lot. From the narrow space between the dumpsters, we watched a silver pickup park in a line with the other two vehicles. The driver stepped down and surveyed each parked car before entering.

A black-and-white unit appeared at the far end of the

alley. Two officers climbed out of the car and ran toward us. Thomas motioned to them to stay low.

"Robbery?" one asked.

"Not sure," Thomas replied. "The building is supposed to be closed. They had a robbery and murder a couple weeks ago that appear to be drug related. At least four inside; one is a health inspector who may be caught in something bigger than he intended."

He pointed at the building. "You take the south side, check for other exit doors, and be ready to go in the front if you hear shots." They both nodded, unstrapped their guns, and ran across the parking lot.

"Laura, wait in my car. It'll be warmer," he said, tossing the keys. "And safer."

# 54

Jake thought Pedro and Michael Lundeen appeared to be at a standoff. Michael wasn't producing the cell phone, which he obviously couldn't do because Laura had put the incriminating phone in his briefcase less than an hour ago. It was stashed in his car sitting in the back of the building. The lie about the lock box key was all Michael had to offer.

And Pedro—whoever he was—wasn't giving any payoff without the phone and the incriminating photos. "*Amigo,* the *jefe,* he no like excuses."

"I don't give a damn what your boss likes, Pedro. I couldn't risk keeping it with me."

Jake heard a gun click. "Then we go now, *amigo.* Where is this box?"

"No way," Michael countered. "I want a head start getting out of town. You take the key, I take the cash, and I'm gone. It's a trust issue, isn't it?" he taunted. "You don't trust me; I don't trust you. You kill me here; somebody else finds the phone. What's it gonna be?"

"Who else find it?"

"Do I look stupid?" Michael challenged. "Let's just say if I don't contact someone within twenty-four hours, that some-one knows to take the duplicate key to the cops."

Realizing he had been holding his breath, Jake let it escape and pushed himself even deeper into the corner.

He heard the back door open a third time.

⤸

As soon as Thomas left, I followed at what I hoped was a discreet and safe distance, intending to use Jake's car as a viewpoint. I watched the cops circle the parked vehicles, check inside each with flashlights, and signal to Thomas. He waited at the back door while they circled around to the front.

Something about the big silver pickup stirred my memory. I closed my eyes to think. Who mentioned it and why? Unable to find an answer, I refocused on the back door and saw Thomas slide inside.

I ran for cover next to the parked vehicles to get a better look at the pickup. I figured if shots erupted, the darkened south side of the building would provide refuge. When I brushed past the back end of the silver truck, my jacket snagged on a ragged edge of the damaged bumper.

As I pried the fabric loose, I read the plate: VWZ-658. Very wild zebras. Kyle's mnemonic. This had to be the truck that had forced him and Darren off the road. Whose was it? And why was he here?

I ran back across the parking lot to the unmarked car and fumbled with the key fob. "Damn it, open." Inside, I looked for the radio switch.

"I'm in Detective Thomas Garcia's car. He needs more backup." I spat the words as fast as they would come.

"Who am I talking to?" the dispatcher asked.

"Laura Neilson. I'm in the alley behind Sir Pedro's restaurant on East Lake Street. There are at least three guys inside, maybe more. Detective Garcia and two cops just went in, but the pickup that just arrived was involved in a hit and run last week."

"Slow down, ma'am, I can't understand you."

"Send backup to Sir Pedro's," I repeated, word for word. Then I opened the glove compartment and removed the gun and ammunition I'd used for target practice.

"What is the address, ma'am?"

I opened the chamber and inserted six bullets.

"Ma'am, are you still there?"

"Not any longer."

I ran across the parking lot and stopped behind the SUV, pointing the gun at the back door.

# 55

After the third person entered, Jake hardly dared to breathe. The conversation got louder. The newcomer was threatening Michael Lundeen, and Jake heard a whack followed by a loud grunt of pain.

"Michael, I must have your cell phone. You know this. Why you try to hide it?" the newcomer threatened.

"Bastard," Michael snarled. "You're not gettin' it unless I get my money. Like I told Pedro here, if we can't come to an agreement, the cops get the key to my box in twenty-four hours."

"You lie."

Jake heard another whack and more groaning.

"Luis, what if he tells the truth?"

"Michael tell the truth?" Luis sneered. "He does not know truth. Do you?"

Jake heard a thud. Michael groaned again.

Jake leaned back and closed his eyes. He was stuck here until the cops came. He didn't dare try sneaking out the back door for fear he'd be caught. And he had Laura to worry about. Had she called Thomas?

The back door opened again.

A shadow moved past the narrow slit of light through the mop closet door. Jake waited to hear another angry voice. Would they kill Michael here or take him some other place for it? After they had his fake key.

"Police! Show me your hands," Thomas yelled.

Jake slid to the floor in gratitude, only to be startled by the sound of gunfire.

He heard glass breaking and more gunshots. He assumed it was cops but didn't know for sure. He heard a loud cry followed by a defeated, painful moan. Someone ran past the mop closet.

⌒

I heard the shots and flattened myself on the wall near the back entrance and waited, holding the gun steady in both hands. Another shot rang out, and the back door flew open. The pickup driver ran to his vehicle, jerked open the door, and scrambled inside.

I aimed at the windshield and pulled the trigger, expecting glass to shatter. Jagged cracks reached outward from the impact, but the glass stayed intact. I fired again. The vehicle propelled backward. I crouched behind the other cars, holding the gun steady.

When the driver's window came down and a weapon appeared, I dropped to the frozen ground, fearing he would track my breath in the frigid air. I kept the gun ready in case he decided to drive closer. Instead, he fired randomly in my direction before racing toward the alley.

Sirens wailed. Red lights danced in the sky like disco balls as more squad cars approached. I stayed down on the pavement.

The back door opened. On my stomach, I steadied my elbows and pointed the gun at the shadowy figure that emerged.

"Laura, where are you? I heard gunshots out here."

"It's a good thing it's you," I called, rising to my knees. "I may only have two bullets left to defend myself."

Thomas came over and extended his hand, pulling me up. "Did he hurt you? Did he fire at you?" His eyes flashed concern. "Are you okay?"

"No, yes, and yes. I hit the windshield twice. But he still drove off."

"He won't get far with that damage."

"Silver pickup truck, license letters VWZ. Sound familiar?"

He paused, nodding his head. "Yeah, it does. Kyle and Darren. It's Luis, their friendly, helpful butcher. He almost killed Michael. The other one inside is Pedro LaPaz, previous owner of this place. He got caught in crossfire."

"And Jake?"

"I didn't see him."

"He's in there someplace, Thomas. How could you not see him? Did you call out for him?"

Thomas ran back to the building with me close behind. "Jake," we called in unison. "Where are you?"

He stuck his head out of a door. "Clear?"

"Hell, yes. Why didn't you call out and let us know where you were?" Thomas snapped. "You could have been shot by the other cops."

"'Cause they both had guns. That's why," Jake growled. "Pedro and Luis. I heard Michael say it was Pedro who hit me. There were too many gunshots. I wasn't sure who came out on top." Jake leaned against a dusty kitchen counter, relieved.

I wanted to hug him but instead sniffed and wrinkled my nose. "Phew. Where have you been?"

"In the lovely mop closet," he grumbled. "Stay back."

We moved aside as two patrol cops led Pedro out the back door in handcuffs. I stepped into the dining room to watch the EMTs attend to Michael. They had already attached IVs to his battered body and were applying a pressure wrap to stop heavy bleeding in his thigh.

Thomas stood behind me and rested his hand on my shoulder. "I was afraid," he said softly. "Luis would have killed you if you tried to block his way. It's why I forgot about Jake."

"I was worried about both of you."

"I'm glad." He let my body lean into his.

"What happened to Lundeen?" Jake came up behind us to watch the paramedics.

"He took a bullet in the melee," Thomas confirmed. "Luis turned and fired in my direction, and Pedro fired at Michael. Then the uniforms busted through the glass doors. Luis fired at them and ran into the kitchen. With three guns pointed at him, Pedro gave up."

"I wasn't sure who came out, but when he opened the truck door, I knew it wasn't you. That's when I shot at him."

"You shot him?" Jake's eyes widened. "Where'd you find a gun?"

"In the glove compartment. The gun was in Thomas's glove compartment."

Jake squinted and looked directly at me. "And?"

"I shot at the truck. Not actually at him."

He glared at me and then at Thomas before announcing, "I'm going home to shower. See you at the office."

"Not quite yet," Thomas informed him. "The investigators will need a full statement. Tonight. And that cell phone you picked up. Sounds like it has photos of Luis killing Javier."

"It can't wait until morning?"

"No, Jake, it can't wait."

Thomas sat in the station lobby while I gave my statement to another investigator. It was almost ten o'clock. He called a black and white to take me home. "I'll see you tomorrow," he promised with a smile.

Home never felt so good. I took a hot shower, brewed a cup of tea, snuggled into my chair with Dude on my lap, and watched an inane late-night talk show to settle my mind.

Dude purred and kneaded my lap and chest and rubbed his head under my chin. I purred back at him, "I love you too, big guy." *Does Thomas make me happy enough to purr?*

# 56

My cell rang at 5:45 a.m.

"It's on the morning news," Jake informed me.

"What is?" I closed my eyes. It was still dark outside, and the bed cocoon wasn't ready to open up after a restless night. "What time is it anyway?"

"It's quarter to six."

"And you're calling me why?"

"Couldn't sleep. Still hearing shots ring out in my head. Can't get rid of the image of Michael all beat up. So I turned on the morning news, and they had brief coverage about Sir Pedro's last night."

I perked up. "How much info did they have? Did they mention Javier?" My mind raced. "Did the cops catch up with Luis?" I stepped into wool slippers, grabbed my robe, and shuffled toward the coffee maker in the kitchen.

"According to the reporter, one man was arrested, that would be Pedro, and another was injured. That would be Michael or whatever his real name is. Police found the pickup truck but not the driver."

I poured water in the machine and dumped coffee

grounds into a filter. "We have to tell Franklin everything this morning. Before he finds out from a different source."

"I'm toast," Jake moaned.

"Not any darker than me. Remember who shot the truck windshield." I drummed my fingers on the counter impatiently as I watched the dark liquid drop into the waiting pot.

"Do you have a license to carry?"

"What do you think?"

"Think Thomas can keep our names out of it?" he asked hopefully.

"Yeah, right." I poured a cup of coffee before it was done dripping and added flavored cream.

"Eight?"

"Eight sharp."

Franklin was sitting at my desk when Jake and I tried to slip into the office.

"I figured you two might be involved. Enlighten me." He handed Jake a can of diet cola. A cup of cappuccino sat on my desk.

"I had a call from a reporter this morning asking if the unidentified health department employee in the raid at Sir Pedro's was one of mine. Of course, I couldn't confirm or deny anything, but I'd certainly like the details." He smiled, but there was no twinkle in his eyes.

After we relocated to a meeting room and closed the door, Jake detailed our stop at Sir Pedro's. "Yes, I know . . . bad decisions."

Franklin looked at me. "And you just stood by as all of this unfolded?"

"I wasn't inside."

"Aha, and what exactly does that imply?" The piercing question punctured my gut. My stomach roiled.

I took a very long swallow of the now-cold coffee. "It implies I stayed near the vehicle as Thomas ordered." A white lie, but it would suffice until I talked to Thomas.

Franklin stood and cast his mountainous shadow over us. "Let me know when you have to testify."

A temporary pardon, as Jake termed the meeting.

Back at my desk, I reviewed our notes from the factory and started a report to attach to the findings George and his team would write. I wasn't sure if he would turn everything over to the Department of Justice for federal prosecution or just recommend heavy fines. I hoped it'd be both.

Other states were investigating similar outbreaks, finding the same salmonella DNA as our cases and the same food source. Statistics to date included eight states; 147 ill, ages ranging from three to eighty-six; nine hospitalized; and four deaths, including the two in Minnesota, a thirty-two-year-old diabetic man in North Dakota, and a six-year-old boy in Iowa. I knew there would be additional illnesses to be documented, many that would never be reported, and perhaps even a death or two never associated with eating a simple potpie.

Baker's Best products were pulled from supermarkets throughout its distribution network. Factory management would be required to provide written responses for corrective actions on every point in the inspection George and his staff performed, to undergo a rigorous inspection before being allowed to reopen, and to expect USDA compliance visits in the following year.

Once again, I felt incredibly sad for the families affected by illness and death and was furious at management who overlooked food safety for profits.

My phone rang. I hoped to hear from Thomas. It wasn't him.

"Hello, Dorothy," I answered. The last time we had talked, she hung up, angry because I couldn't provide immediate information for her lawyer. What would it be today?

"I have a new lawyer," she announced in her usual monotone. "He wants to know how soon he can get a final report."

"Please have him call me, Dorothy. I can give him preliminary information today."

"Why couldn't you do it the last time I called?" Her words spit venom.

I choked back a retort. "Because we hadn't concluded the inspections. What happened to your other lawyer?"

"Peter Born found out he was a fraud. Like all men who say they can help."

*How does she categorize Peter? He's a man who helped.*

"Dorothy, I can give you very good support references for abused women." Not waiting for her refusal, I continued. "I know firsthand what you've been through. I accepted help to recover. You should too."

Silence.

I waited.

Then sniffing and blowing.

"Dorothy, it's okay. Let me call someone to help you. Please." I leaned back in my chair and closed my eyes. An old vision returned. "Please let me help you," I begged.

She blew her nose again and coughed. "Maybe."

After reciting contact phone numbers, which she said she'd look into, I called Rose and Peter Born. Holding the phone six inches from my ear, I listened to Peter repeat the information to Rose. They were eager to help.

"Do you think she should stay in her house?" Rose took over the phone.

"It depends on what Dorothy wants. Right now she needs to talk to a therapist."

"We'll make sure she does," Rose confirmed.

"I'll follow up with you and her next week. Thank you for this, Rose. You've just saved her in ways you won't ever fully appreciate." I knew Dorothy would be in good hands.

Ugly memories came racing back. I thought about Thomas. *How well do I really know him? Is he angry I used his gun to shoot the silver truck? Will he lash out when he calls?*

*Stop. This kind of thinking puts me in the same boat as Dorothy, not trusting or believing any man. I do trust him. Yes, I trusted before, but that was a different situation. Right?*

Maybe.

# 57

Thomas took Michael's cell phone to the lab and watched the short video taken the night Javier was murdered. The audio was muddy and faint, but the techs assured him they'd do their magic to enhance it. The time and date on the video coincided with Javier's murder. Two men were pushing each other when one of them—Thomas assumed it was Javier—pulled a weapon out of his belt but lost it. The other man, Luis, picked up the gun and aimed at Javier. A shot could be heard. Then silence.

Thomas was anxious to question Michael as soon as doctors gave the okay. The faster he could be moved to a jail cell, the safer he would be. Thomas was certain there was already someone assigned to silence him. Possibly even Luis himself would attempt it. His truck was abandoned three blocks from Sir Pedro's. Police had searched a fifteen-block area without luck. Luis had faded into the Latino neighborhood without a shadow.

Thomas reread Jake's statement. Michael had claimed someone else had a key to a lock box. Obviously, it was a lie, but Thomas worried Luis would be looking for that someone.

The first person coming to mind was Sheila because she appeared to be the one person Michael might trust. All his other contacts were just like him, liars and thieves. Thomas called Robbinsdale police, requesting a watch on her for at least forty-eight hours. The county sheriff already had Luis's meat market and his residence under surveillance.

Thomas called the hospital. The physician on duty confirmed Michael Lundeen could be questioned but needed at least another day to recover before being transported to jail. He was still hooked to the IV stand. Thomas worried staying in the hospital left him vulnerable in spite of 24/7 protection. Luis was desperate to find the cell phone video.

My inspection schedule for the day included a McDonalds, a Greek restaurant, Pizza by the Slice, and an ice cream shop. The last inspection for the afternoon was a Mexican restaurant called Tejas Tacos Buffet, only five blocks from Sir Pedro's. After last night, the entire neighborhood felt sinister, crushed by heavy dark clouds and impending danger.

I opted for street parking and walked cautiously on the partially shoveled sidewalk toward the entrance, slipping once but catching my balance before hitting the cold concrete. A rush of warm, hot-pepper-infused air enveloped me when I opened the back door. I sneezed.

The cook nodded in recognition and left to find Alejandro while I hung my coat and prepared for the inspection.

Alejandro had been a fixture in this area for many years. A tall, slender Latino with disheveled graying hair, he had dark eyes that sparkled with curiosity and joy. He'd built his business from scratch, and I've kidded him many times about his buffet bunker. It was at least five feet wide and eight feet long, built with concrete block and sided with decorative blue and yellow tiles made in his hometown. The pans were filled with taco fixings, salad greens, peppers, cheeses, and salsas for every taste. It was always fiesta time at Tejas.

Maybe it was the time of day, or the events at Sir Pedro's the previous night, or just the weather, but Alejandro definitely was not in a good mood.

"This is not a good time," he said with unusual bluntness. "We are too busy, and I don't have time to walk with you. Come back tomorrow." His dark eyes were not smiling.

This was not at all like Alejandro. He had an excellent working relationship with our department. His restaurant always scored near the top, and he welcomed our visits. Today he was edgy and seemed nervous. Was he hiding something? Were the refrigerators down? Was the dishwasher out of commission?

"Alejandro, you know I can't do that. If you don't have time, I'll just do the inspection without you and give you a breakdown before I leave." I turned on the computer and walked to the hand sink.

"No," he emphasized. "Today is not good for me. Please?"

"Alejandro, the inspection needs to be done. I'm here, and I'm doing it. Now." I jammed a paper hand towel in the wastebasket and picked up my computer.

Before he could provide a rebuttal, my cell rang. Thomas.

"Excuse me a moment. I need to take this." I walked to a back corner for privacy. "What's up?"

"I questioned Michael this afternoon. He's a loser that got

greedy. Trying to blackmail a drug dealer is not a smart move. He should have stuck with petty theft of cleaning supplies. We're transferring him to a jail cell tonight for his security. One of our sources reports Luis has a contract out on him."

"Where is Luis?"

"We know he's still in Minneapolis. The same source says he's waiting for a contact to show up and fly him out. We have the small county airports covered. We're closer to locating him, and that's all I can say for now."

"Is Jake in any danger?" I whispered, looking up to see Alejandro glaring.

"He didn't see anything, so no. He may not even have to appear in court." Then he asked, "Where are you?"

"Tejas Tacos, East Twenty-sixth Street."

"Only six blocks from Sir Pedro's, right?"

"Five, actually."

"Laura," he shouted loud enough to make me jump. "I don't like this at all. Luis is still around, we know he's got a weapon, and if he listens to the news, he knows inspectors were involved last night. Are you driving a state car?"

"Yes, I am. Thomas, stop making a big deal about it. He never saw me, and I wouldn't be able to pick him out in a lineup. I need to get back to work."

⸻

Thomas looked at the disconnected call in disbelief. "Damn it. What the hell is she thinking?"

He punched her phone number and listened to it roll to voice message. He didn't often feel fear, but this was different. Everything felt wrong.

# 58

After making apologies to Alejandro, I repeated that he did not need to accompany me on the inspection.

Shaking his head, he again indicated an unwillingness to let me continue. "This is not a good time, Laura."

"Ah, come on, Alejandro. Do I have to come back with a cop to do an inspection? What exactly is going on here?"

A waiter pushed open the swinging door from the dining room, hustling past us to pick up an order. The pleasant chatter of diners slid in with his air of efficiency. Pans clattered on the range, and Mexican music danced from a little black radio at the end of the taco prep workstation.

Deep in thought, Alejandro surveyed his kitchen from one side to the other before speaking. "Okay. We do the kitchen."

While I scanned the cook's hot holding log, he alluded to news about the previous evening. "I don't want customers to think we are all drug dealers. Pedro, he was a bad actor. He made bad friends."

"How did that happen?" I stuck a thermometer into a pan of shredded pork on the steam table.

"Bad friends," he repeated, denying me further information.

"Pork is one hundred forty-one degrees. Excellent."

We stepped into the walk-in cooler. I stuck the probe into beans, cooked rice, and taco meat. All temperatures were fine.

"Can I see your cooling logs?" I asked when we left the cold storage box.

"Yes, I have logs in the office. I will get them in a minute. Wait here," he answered as he walked toward two waiters in a heated argument.

Spanish flowed fast and furious. The small, chubby waiter pointed to the dining room, vigorously shaking his finger. I picked up a few words but couldn't follow the conversation until I heard *restaurante del Pedro* and *el jefe*. Sir Pedro's and the boss? Which boss?

*Or maybe it's just street gossip. But why is he so animated?*

Alejandro spoke quietly, calming both men. When he returned to continue our inspection, I asked, "Was that about last night?"

"Yes." He cleared this throat. "They, ah, are worried about getting arrested because they are Mexican."

Something in his voice told me this wasn't the truth. "That's not likely," I said. "Unless they're selling drugs." He had no reaction. "Who is *el jefe*?" I tried to sound as disinterested as possible.

Alejandro stopped dead. I could tell he was considering his reply. "I am *el jefe* here," he said at last. "I am the boss."

It was pretty darn obvious he wasn't going to tell me anything. His sudden evasiveness made me wonder if he was involved with the drug trade after all. I wanted to believe Alejandro was one of the good guys.

"Shall we check the buffet next?" I asked. "After that, I'll look at the cooling logs and then we'll be done."

"Well," he paused, "maybe not this time. There is only a little food out there now."

I knew the buffet was always set up. By this hour, pans of taco condiments were nearly overflowing in anticipation of the early evening diners. What exactly was going on? Was the cooling unit broken, and he was afraid I'd throw out lukewarm food?

"That's okay," I confirmed, walking toward the dining room door. "I'll just check what's there and then be done. It won't take long at all."

"*Es* not necessary," he almost begged. When he grabbed my arm, I jerked it away.

"What's wrong, Alejandro?" I stared into his dark eyes, looking for some truth.

"Everyone is very nervous. They heard about the inspector at Sir Pedro's. Now they think any inspector is not safe in their business. One man is still not arrested. We are all, ah, edgy."

"Do you know where the man is?"

"Oh, no. No, we do not," he answered, looking at the floor.

"Do you know who he is?"

Alejandro's face was the color of fresh guacamole. "No, I do not."

"Then there's nothing to worry about. This will take less than five minutes, and then I'll be gone and not return for about six months." I pushed the swinging door open into the dining room.

~

Thomas answered the call as his car approached an intersection. "Yeah, tell me something good." He listened. "You're sure? Just one vehicle? How many passengers?"

He turned on the flashing red lights. "I'm three blocks away."

Luis's contact had just parked in front of Tejas Tacos.

# 59

I pulled out my thermometer and started to record temperatures of the buffet foods. Alejandro hovered just behind, surveying his dining room, focusing on a particular booth in the back corner.

My caution meter jumped to one hundred. Rather than be obvious and turn around to stare at the booth, I moved to the other side of the buffet where I could steal a look. The customer in the booth moved out of view.

As I was recording temperatures, the front door opened with a rush of cold air escorting a short, stocky man wearing a cowboy hat low over his eyes and a heavy leather sheepskin-lined jacket. In some parts of the state, this attire wouldn't raise an eyebrow. In Minneapolis, it was unusual. I glanced up to see him walking directly to the back booth.

Alejandro leaned into my ear, whispering, "You must go. It is too dangerous."

Nodding in agreement, I closed the computer and stuffed my thermometer in a pocket. Just as we turned to leave, Thomas came in the front door. He came directly to us. "Laura, we have to leave. Now."

The man in the Stetson was staring at us. Without a warning, Alejandro pushed me down on the floor. A shot rang out. Then another and another, shattering the beautiful buffet tiles, cracking the concrete blocks. Thomas pointed his Glock at the booth. Customers screamed and crawled under tables. Chairs flew across the floor. A lone woman ran out the front door, escaping into the cold November evening.

Alejandro fell on top of me. As I struggled to move him off my back, he rolled over, bleeding heavily. His warm blood soaked through my clothes and was dripping onto the floor. He moaned as I tried to pull him closer to the buffet fortress.

A waiter cracked open the kitchen door behind us. Bullets burned through the flimsy wood.

"Luis," Thomas shouted. "More police are on the way. Make it easy on yourself and give up."

More shots. The light above the buffet exploded, spewing glass on us. One bullet hit a stainless pan of hot frijoles sitting on the buffet ledge. Pinto beans flew in the air. I ducked to escape the burning spatters, only to find more blood. Alejandro was now on his hands and knees, his head bent down, panting. I couldn't see where the blood was coming from. Then he collapsed, and I saw the large red patch on his shoulder. I touched his neck. He had a pulse.

Assessing the situation, Thomas whispered, "There are two of them. I'll try to distract them. Find something to stop the bleeding."

"Are you crazy? Where?" My heart pounded in my ears.

"Napkins. Now, " he ordered, and shot at the corner booth.

Adrenaline kicked in. I reached up, grabbed a pile of

napkins from the buffet counter, pulled them down, and began packing them into Alejandro's wound. Another bullet splintered the kitchen door behind us, and a second one exploded a pan of taco shells.

Loud gasping sobs came from terrified customers. Followed by silence. The shooting had stopped.

"What's going on?" I whispered.

"Reloading? Calling in reinforcements?" he speculated. Thomas kept his weapon pointed at the corner booth. Waiting.

I shivered. The front door had not closed after Thomas entered, and now freezing air blew over us like a premonition of death.

Seconds later, I heard the joyous sounds of sirens echoing off the city streets and saw red flashing lights pulsing through the dusk. Through the open front door, I spotted a cop running to the entrance, gun ready. More shots erupted on the street. The cop stopped to look back, then continued in our direction. Thomas made some hand signals, and the cop waited just outside.

"Throw down the weapons," he yelled. "We have your *amigos* surrounded. There's no way out." The cop in the doorway nodded in our direction. Thomas nodded in return. He shouted again, this time in Spanish.

Silence.

Abruptly, a firestorm of bullets hit the walls behind us. They were closer, more threatening. Thomas ordered, "Crawl into the kitchen. Now."

My hand slipped in the blood before my pant knees could soak it up. The shooting continued. I reached for the door and pushed it inward. A large hand grabbed mine and pulled. The cop didn't stop until we were out of the bullet trajectories.

Surveying the blood on my hands and clothes, he said, "EMTs are in the back. Can you walk okay?"

Before I could answer, three other cops in vests and helmets rushed past us through the shattered door. I heard two more shots, followed by the loud voices of police giving orders.

"There's a man in there," I said, pointing to the dining room, "who needs help right now." I turned to take him to Alejandro. Instead, he picked me up and carried me out the back door.

"Let's take care of you first."

Two ambulances and a fire truck were parked on a side street, waiting for casualties. An EMT rushed toward us. "Need a gurney?"

"No, dammit, it's not my blood. It's from the guy inside. His name is Alejandro."

He brushed past us and ran toward the restaurant. Another checked me over anyway and determined exactly what I'd told him.

A TV van parked across the street. I looked at my watch. *Yeah, this will make the six o'clock news. But I'm not going to be part of it.*

I needed my coat and purse with the car keys. They were in the restaurant kitchen, near the back door. The cop inside informed me it was a crime scene and I couldn't retrieve anything, not even the key to my apartment.

Shivering in falling temperatures, I begged, "At least let me warm up inside until I can get a ride."

He looked at my bloodstained clothes. "Lady, you seen the EMT yet?"

Before I could answer, Thomas opened the shattered dining room door. He stopped dead and stared. "Laura, are you hurt?"

"I'm fine, Thomas. Please tell this nice young officer I just need my coat and my purse so I can go home and get out of here."

He nodded to the officer.

Thomas held my coat, asking again, "You're not hurt, right?"

"No," I confirmed. "What happened in there?"

"Luis is dead. The cowboy is on his way to the hospital without his Stetson. We have the driver of the escape car in a squad."

"Do you think I could have my computer too? Or is it part of the crime scene?" I zipped up my coat and pulled on a stocking hat.

"I'll get it to you tomorrow. Promise."

"Franklin would like that."

⤸

After stuffing all my bloodstained clothes into a trash bag, I took a hot shower; slipped into flannel pajamas, a big fluffy robe, and warm slippers; and shuffled to the kitchen for tea and toast. Nothing else was appealing. Dude sensed not all was well and curled up on the sofa.

Jake had left three voice messages of increasing urgency. He'd watched a live newsfeed from Tejas Tacos and feared I was somewhere nearby. I figured it was time to call him before the late news stations had even more information and he was pounding on my door.

"You weren't near the restaurant in the news, were you? It looked scary as hell. Was Thomas involved? Was it Luis? Got any idea what happened there? I've been worried," he babbled.

"I assumed it from your phone calls, Jake. Yes, Thomas was there, and Luis was there, and Luis is dead. And the owner of the business was badly injured in the gunfire."

"You know this because you might possibly have been there with him? Or just had a recent update from him?"

"I was in the wrong place at the wrong time."

I started the story from the beginning.

# 60

"Flowers," Thomas said, handing me a large bouquet of yellow mums and white carnations and a bottle of chilled prosecco.

I closed the apartment door, hung his jacket, and took the unexpected offerings. "And the occasion is?"

"Administrative leave, vacation, mental health break. Pick one. In any case, I won't be getting any calls tonight needing immediate attention."

"I can live with that. I'm on leave for five days. Franklin insisted. Jake's jealous because he didn't get any time after the night at Sir Pedro's. And I suppose the three of us will have a big, heated discussion about where I can and cannot inspect. They're both overprotective."

Thomas frowned but refrained from offering his viewpoint when I frowned back.

"Tell me what will happen to Michael Lundeen," I asked, changing the subject.

"He'll go to trial for stealing the chemicals. He could plead guilty, but I suspect he's afraid of jailhouse justice and thinks he could delay jail time with a jury trial. Luis had contacts everywhere." Thomas reached into the cupboard and removed two glasses.

"What I don't get is why Luis would wait in a restaurant to be picked up. Did he think someone wouldn't call the police? Alejandro knew who he was, I'd bet on it." I opened a pantry door and pulled out a container of mixed nuts.

"Luis has a network in the drug community. If Alejandro had ratted, he'd be looking over his shoulder the rest of his life."

"Have any of his gang members been found, or did they dissolve into the night?"

"Got one, two being pursued." He started to ease the cork off between his thumbs. "DEA is on it now. Ready for bubbly?"

"Yes, thanks."

"What about the potpie mess?" he asked after the cork popped.

"My part's done. If the department gets any more complaints, the epi staff will conduct the necessary interviews. Jake still has statistical work to finish. But, yeah, we're pretty much done. USDA is recommending both Michael and the company president be brought to trial. Last I heard from Sheila, the plant's being purchased by another processor. Heads have rolled in the Ohio offices, but they can still be held liable."

"Will you be called to testify?"

"Doubtful. We've sent our reports to the feds, and they'll assemble everything for the trial. It likely won't be for almost a year, which takes way too long to my way of thinking, but that's the system. Can you reach the vase up there, on the top shelf?" I pointed.

While I cut the stems and stuck the flowers in the vase, Dude appeared and rubbed his chin on Thomas's leg, purring loudly enough for us to laugh.

"How's Alejandro?" he asked, reaching down to stroke the cat's head.

"Out of intensive care. Some of his employees have started cleaning up the mess and making repairs. Customers started a GoFundMe account to help him. I expect his buffet will be rebuilt as sturdy as ever. A toast to the buffet." I laughed, pinging our glasses.

"Can we talk?" he asked.

I nodded.

I knew what was coming. I'd lost sleep examining all possible scenarios, questioning myself over and over. And I knew what my answer would be.

We sat on the sofa. Dude jumped between us, rolled on his back, and waited for attention.

"It's about the dating manual," Thomas began. "Are you good with it? Because I am. Can we try?"

I rubbed Dude's belly.

"I've put a lot of thought into this, Thomas. I asked myself a lot of questions. Are you safe? Can I trust you? How do you control anger? Are you truthful?"

"And?" he asked, looking into my eyes for an answer.

"Yeah, let's give the manual a try."

Dude jumped on my lap and purred a concerto of approval.

Don't miss B. J. Packer's next novel:

# Deadly Revenge

# 1

"Close the door, Laura," Franklin Hamilton ordered, his mouth set in a tight-lipped grimace.

I pushed it with my elbow and sat in the chair opposite the manager of food safety for the Minnesota Health Department. Generally, this mountain of a man was in good spirits and loved to mix a lot of sports analogies in his discussions. But not this morning. April showers spattered the window, gray overcast left no shadows. His demeanor said there was a problem.

"I want you to do a critical inspection of the kitchen in Golden Oaks Nursing Home. As soon as we're finished here." He leaned back in his chair tenting his fingers in frustration.

"But we don't go into nursing homes," I protested, and quickly ate those words. "At least not until today."

"I need someone in there who's discreet and won't ruffle too many feathers." He gave me the steely football stare I'd seen before. It meant stay focused, do your job, and don't leave any holes in the line.

"Yes, sir."

"The nursing home director called me late last night.

They have at least forty of their hundred-plus residents ill with diarrhea and vomiting, and seven are in the hospital. They've isolated the sick, but she thinks it must be coming from the kitchen."

He went on to explain he had met Jessica Hartley on a nursing home task force the past winter, and they had worked together on training standards for senior care kitchen employees. He respected her judgement.

And right now, she needed help. None of her kitchen employees were ill. None of the nurses were sick. It didn't seem like a virus. She was sure it had to be the food. She was afraid several patients would die.

"This is the game plan." He shoved a paper over the desk. "Get the roster of all the resident names and phone numbers sent back here ASAP. We'll use the grad student interns to interview as many as we can. Someone from Epidemiology will bring stool kits to the home later this morning. I want you to interview every kitchen employee and go over every single piece of equipment and procedure with a magnifying glass. Take swabs and food samples. Talk to the nurses about onset times. Keep me updated."

As I rose to leave, he added, "I have a bad feeling about this outbreak. It scares the hell out of me."

CPSIA information can be obtained
at www.ICGtesting.com
Printed in the USA
LVHW050148010523
745722LV00005B/395